Charli

Luis Martinez

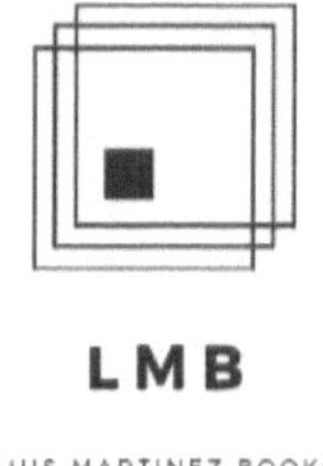

LMB

LUIS MARTINEZ BOOKS

Charli

By Luis Martinez

Copyright © 2019 by LUIS MARTINEZ BOOKS

ISBN: 9781734334609

Contents

Reflections

I am beautiful. My mirror tries to remind me of that as I stare at myself in silence every morning when I get ready to start my day. Although at times many of my choices of the past have made me feel ugly inside, I still remind myself every day that I am beautiful. Nothing about it will ever take how I feel physically away from me. I have truly been blessed good looks. Even though being beautiful can be a blessing to most, I feel that I have also been cursed with having a *badass* looking body to go along with it. Mostly everywhere I go, I get stared at by all types of men. Please understand, I am not trying to be conceded. In fact, being beautiful with a nice body is what has made it very difficult for me to distinguish the difference between truly being loved from not knowing if a man just wants to fuck me.

I'm sure that I am not the only woman who feels this way. This has been the case for many other beautiful women across the world. The things that most men whisper in my ear are usually the things that I do want to hear. The way they have touched me and the way that they have held me has made me feel like I am wanted. But in the end, I believe that it has always been my own insecurities that have affected me after being disappointed so many times that brings out the ugly in me. My fear of making the wrong decisions in the past continue to haunt me and keeps me from giving a man all of me.

I really can't place all the blame and how I feel towards being in a relationship on men. I would love for one day to find a man that not only sees the woman that I see in the mirror, but also feels lucky to be the one to have me in his arms. I wish that I could find the kind of love that would erase all of my negative thoughts and all of the lies that I have been misled by. I don't want to forever think or feel that all men are alike. I also have to take some of the blame for making myself so vulnerable to what I have always been attracted to. Maybe it is the places where I choose to hang out and have a good time that attracts the wrong men. In fact, it could just be all me. Sometimes I sit there and wonder if because I am in such a rush to find happiness that maybe I have turned them all off and driven them all away.

So far, I have only run into the types of men that have weakened me to the point where I have just fallen for lies that drew only the illusions of what I have always wanted. Relationships have become harder and much more difficult for me because I don't want to be that scorned woman who takes it out on every man that could possibly be the one for me. These days, it's just not easy to trust or feel secure enough where you can just trust anyone. In fact, every time I see or hear about relationships, it seems as though the *side-piece* is having a better relationships with other women's boyfriends than they are.

One thing that I have learned about men is that they have all the time in the world to come up with the most creative things to say to a woman. Especially when he has his mind made up that he wants to fuck her. We, as women, take forever to get dressed, do our hair, put on make-up, and at times even force ourselves to put on the tightest clothes just to look good. And as long as all that takes, all they want to do is unbutton my jeans or lift my sundress up from behind as soon as their dicks get hard. Even though my intentions are not to go out and look for a man, my presence sort of attracts them to come and talk to me. They smile, they offer me drinks, they ask me to dance. Yeah, all the great things that I wish someone who truly loved me would offer and be real about. But, how do I know I when I would be turning down the right one? Could it be that the men that I am attracted to is my problem? Could it be that the one who smiles and offers me a drink but doesn't make a move be the one that I should be attracted to and focusing on? I don't know. I'm so confused. It does suck at times to be beautiful.

When I was a younger, I can remember picturing myself being in love and walking down the aisle with the man who would be with me forever. Being home, cooking, cleaning and of course, taking great care of my husband. In fact, I did get married at a very young age to a man who I thought was going to be my everything. But that didn't last too long. We had a baby girl together. Not to get all into that, but I wanted you to know that I was ready to be with one man and one man only for the rest of my life. My intentions were never to be where I am today. Since our divorce, my life has been nothing but a roll-a-coaster.

Our divorce made me feel like I had to start all over again, but now I had a daughter. All I could think about was her growing up trying to figure out why her daddy and I weren't together. Aside from trying to figure that out, I now had to be very careful of any man that I would bring into my world. And that was the beginning of my dark stage. That's when I began to chase after the happiness that I thought I had when I first got married.

Today, I still feel beautiful. I'm just not as happy as I once was. It has become very confusing for me because I know what I want, I know what I need. I sometimes even feel that I know what a man wants and what he needs. But I am just not sure if it's my looks and my body that attracts them my way or if it's my weakness that allows them to feel comfortable enough to continue lying to me only to get what they want. A broken heart comes with many consequences. It weakens you no matter how strong you try to be. Unfortunately for me, it has made me feel very insecure. Since my divorce, I have come across a few men who I have gone out on dates with who seem to give me a little motivation and sometimes feel as if I could maybe give a little more of myself to them. About a week or two into it, something that they say or do only reminds me of situations that I have already dealt with before. And that right there is my problem. Not just my problem, but I also feel that's the problem with most of us as women. This is my love struggle.

The Beast

Along with my beauty comes the beast that all my bad choices of the past have created. In fact, I sometimes feel like it's that ugly beast in me that might have scared away the right person who was probably meant for me. I know for sure that I might have turned off many men because of my attitude and stand-offish ways. I know it's not their fault. But I just don't want to be bothered sometimes. If I wanted to have sex every day I would just stay home and play with myself. Not to be so straight forward, but what's the difference between me doing it to myself from a man who just wants to fuck? Why does he deserve all the pleasure to himself? It sucks that I have to feel this way. I wish that there was a way for us as women to be able to tell a good man from someone who just wants to add another name to their list.

Man, and speaking about that list, I know that my name is probably on a list that have other women that can't even be compared to me. I know for sure that I have probably stood right next to some of them while dancing on the same dance floors or eating at the same restaurants that they have taken me to. I can't even imagine the names and faces that most of these men have slept with, never mind being on that same *fuck* list. Aside from me giving myself to the few men that I have been with, the last thing that I have ever wanted to know about were the women that they have fucked.

The sad thing is that in most cases, you will probably never really know. On some occasions I have heard rumors of some of the women that someone I was messing around with had slept with in the past and it made me feel as though he had no boundaries when it came to the women he chose to be with. Because I know that from the woman that I see in my mirror every morning that none of them compared in any way, shape or form to me. And I mean those three things literally.

Most of them would have denied it anyway so I wouldn't even bother with wasting my time trying to ask them about what the hell they were thinking. And I probably didn't want to know anyway because it would have probably turned me off anyway. Funny how when the tables are turned and they find out about who you have been with though. Because then it's, "You fucked with that bitch-ass nigga?" Yet, I always kept my mouth shut when it came to the monsters that I had heard they had slept with. But in a man's world, the only thing that mattered to them was what a woman had done in her past. He could have fucked over a hundred women, but if he ever heard anything about a woman's past, it was almost as if that was all the info he needed to decide whether you were going to be his woman or just a straight fuck for the night. Not that it really ever mattered to them anyway. Because even if you were labeled a hoe, they would still want to get their dicks wet regardless.

You have no idea how many of those types of men I've had to dodge almost every day so that I wouldn't end up being classified as a hoe like most of the other women have. I never wanted to be labeled as being easy. And all it would have taken was just one single time for me to have fucked the wrong man and the entire city would have thought differently of me. Although it was just that one man, once your name is associated with him, you'll forever be known as a hoe in their eyes. Yet, even that won't stop them from trying to get with you. They'll talk shit about you every chance they could, but once they saw you in public and they had a little liquor in their system, they would try to push up on you like it was guaranteed pussy for the night.

A man can do everything and anything that a woman better not ever dare do. Yet, they want to do to every woman what a woman would be judged for if she did it herself. In other words, in my mind, most of them are pigs. Not all, but I honestly believe that we as women want to do the same things that they think about, but only with one man. They just want it all. I'm not judging all men, but I feel like it is true that when the lights go out, all they care about is *bussin' a nut*. They usually regret it the next day, but in the meantime, while they are fuckin' their little monsters, they just close their eyes and picture someone else who they would rather be fuckin' just to cum and then come up with every excuse to leave right after they are done. And in most cases, you can always tell who those men were because they always walked around the bar acting really *thirsty*.

Around last call at the bar, you will slowly begin to see people making their way towards the exit. I myself was always one of them. As soon as they announced last call, I would guzzle down my drink and wanted to make it to my car as quickly as possible. I usually knew most of the people at every bar or club that I went to so there were barely ever any plans for me once we were done partying. By the end of the night though, there were times that I could have probably fucked the entire crowd of men if I had fallen for each one of them who offered to pay for a drink. Which is one of the reasons why I barely ever accepted any offers or turned them down when they asked me to dance. I always knew what most of them wanted in return by the end of the night. And you could always tell when they thought they had you reeled in. Once they felt that they had you where they wanted you, they barely moved around the bar anymore. They hung around close enough to where they can see you and close enough for you to see that they had no other intentions with any other women. Funny how they think we're all stupid. Because any time before that, you would see them bouncing all over the place or on the dance floor leaning into every other woman's ear trying to say some bullshit that most of us have already heard a million times before.

So, getting back to how you could almost tell who the nasty men were from the ones who were either in relationships or just didn't want to waste their time playing games. If you ever stood around long enough, you would be able to see the ones who were in the parking lot until they were the last ones there. They were usually the nasty ones who would take anything and anyone home that night. They didn't care who it was. Then, after duckin' phone calls all week from the ones they took home the past weekend, now they're walking around all pissed off because the chick keeps stalking them at the bar all night. That's usually the reason why you usually ended up seeing many bar fights breaking out. There was always a chance that two women usually wound up fighting over the same dick that didn't belong to either one of them.

And this was usually where most of us women always thought we were going to find love. Looking back, I always wondered why I never said yes to the men who tried talking to me in normal places? Places like grocery stores or anywhere just out and about besides a bar. Although we really hate to admit it, we as women are naturally attracted to the *bad boys*. We know that they are no good. But the good ones seem boring and always want to do all the right things all the time. I always wanted someone who was edgy and fought back. Not someone who was afraid to lose me and walked on eggshells around me. I have to admit, I can be a bitch sometimes. And with my looks and my body, I can use it all just to piss any man off that I dated.

I didn't have to fight or argue all the time. I would just wait until it was around eight or nine o'clock at night and just start getting ready. After some of our really heated arguments, I would just walk into the bathroom, take a quick shower, and then walk right out in front of him with just my towel on. If he didn't follow me into my room and tried ripping my towel off and just fuck me to make up, I would carry on and pull out my make-up box. Now I would do all of that to see if he would just try to talk to me and work things out. But once I realized that it was going to be one of those nights where neither one of us were going to be speaking to each other, I would go in my closet and grabbed the *slutiest* outfit that I could find, put it on and walk right out the front door without saying a word. That was his last chance. If he didn't come running to the car to try and stop me, then I would just drive to one of my girlfriend's house, park my car where he couldn't see it and just stay there until late that night to make him think I was out fucking somebody else. If he didn't call or text me, I would just sleep there and come back the next day in borrowed pajamas acting like nothing ever happened.

Now that situation could have always gone two different ways. If he had come chasing after me before I drove off, I would feel ok because it would prove that he cared and didn't want me to leave while I was upset. It's not like I really had plans to go anywhere anyway. I was just acting like I was going to go out and have a good time just to piss him off. You know, the stupid little things we do when we think we have a little *pussy power*. But if he did try to stop me, I would put up a fight so that he wouldn't feel like he just won by keeping me home. After doing that a few times, I got tired of playing that game. Because after a while, it was he who started walking out on me. The big difference, he actually never made it back home for a few days. Then, out of nowhere, he began doing it even when we weren't arguing. By then, I knew that he was fed up with my bullshit. It was only a matter of time before I knew I would end up losing him.

I wasn't always like that. I learned that stupid behavior as it became a defense mechanism that I would try to use on the ones that I thought would be afraid to lose me. But, because of the games I've played, I soon found out that most of them just really didn't give a fuck after a while. I have lost quite a few good men because of all the things that other men have put me through. See, in the beginning it's a little cute to them when you're somewhat of a drama queen. You just had to know when to use it and when to stop. Because after six months, it didn't matter that you had the biggest ass, the big tits or even the best pussy. Some of us as women never realize that when we're constantly pissing off a man that we begin to lose our value like a brand-new car being driven out of a dealership. Once they reached that point, your pretty face no longer mattered to them. And that's where I just began to lose it. The more people I was having sex with, the lesser I began to feel like love had anything to do with it. I had to learn the hard way that I had to find a balance between my drama and sex. Too much of both would always drive a man away. Because just like a big dick isn't everything, neither is our pussy and pretty face.

Who's the Bitch

There were times when I caught myself moaning so hard that I felt like a prisoner to my man. I only wanted him to see me that weak as a woman. I fell for him so hard that I did everything in my power just to keep him happy. Anything that he asked for I would just give in. There were times I wanted to give him more, but I didn't want him to feel like most men do when you do certain things for them. You see, I have always heard that men love a woman to be really freaky. But I have also heard that they begin to feel as you have always been doing those things with other men. Men are very weird like that. It could be your very first time ever doing something that you just happen to get caught up in the moment in doing and only wanting to do it for them, next thing you know, after an argument or two, they are now calling you a bitch and a nasty hoe. I know because I have also heard them talk about a woman who just lays there too and just takes it without throwing it back. They just don't know what they want. If you give them too much, you're nasty. If you just lay there, you're boring. Makes you want to just tell them that your moans aren't real and that the orgasms were faked. But what do they care? All they want is to get their quick nut in, roll over and go to sleep like the little babies that they are.

It's crazy to me because you start thinking back at all the nice things that they say to you when they first meet you and how much they are so different from other men and then *boom*, out of nowhere, you ain't shit. It has always been like that with men. Not just with the men that I have been with, but I have also heard many of my girlfriends complaining about the same exact things. And we go through all that drama with them until they see or hear that you were being friendly with another man. Then, they have the nerve to call us a *bitch*. It's like they don't want or need you around, but the moment they feel intimidated by another man, suddenly, you can't go out by yourself and he even tries to control what you can wear in public. And here I am thinking I'm the one with insecurity issues.

Men don't realize that we as women are simple. We seem crazy at times, but we want the same exact things that a man wants. We just want it a lot more than they do. We want it forever, they want it until they cum. We want almost every day to be eventful. We picture everything in colors while all men do is picture everything in black and white. We want the flowers, we want the love, and we crave *a lot* of attention. And if we are there in front of you every single day, we want you to at least put in a little effort. I am tired of dealing with men who only put in the effort when they sense that they are about to lose you. That shit drives me insane. Like, why couldn't you do all the things that you are doing now when I wanted and needed you to? Why is it that suddenly you want to kiss me and fuck me every day and night? And then, once you give them another opportunity to make things right, they get comfortable and start calling you all kinds of *bitches* and *hoes* all over again.

The Freak'n Me

There were those nights at the bar that I felt and looked so good that I just knew I was *killin em'*. I would flirt a bit sometimes just see if I still had it. And as much as I didn't want to mislead anyone, it boosted my ego and hid most of my insecurities. In fact, I knew that I drove some of them crazy with how perfect my ass looked in my tight jeans and how I pushed my tits up a little higher than usual where I left them no other choice but to just go home and play with their dick. Or, they probably fucked their girls a little harder than usual that night thinking about me. Come to think about it, now I even wonder if they were doing me the same way when they came over after being out all night. But I always knew when I really had them because in the middle of the night, I would sometimes get those "*Hey, are you still up*" messages in my inbox that I never ever responded to. Going to the local bars was my thing. It felt good making those men want me, and although I went home alone most of the time, I sometimes wished that I would have found someone to just come over and make me laugh. But, as we all know, those kinds of men were either gay or were very rare. Even when I did find a cute one to just chill with, somehow someway, he would always fuck things up when I told him I was getting tired and needed to go to sleep.

Once a man notices that it's getting later, they never seem to realize that if they really wanted to see me coming out of my *panties* that all they had to do was act like a gentleman and maybe just give me a little kiss on my forehead at the door and say, "have a good night *beautiful*". Now that would make me a lot more curious and maybe even have me fuck his head up a little more by raising their chances of having a second date. But of course, and like in many cases, they always seemed to screw that up for themselves. Once they saw you yawn once, they would ask where your bathroom was just to go freshen up as if they just knew we were going to get some pussy. I knew that because many times, they would come right out and you never even heard the toilet being flushed. All you heard was a little water running as if maybe they were washing their dicks in the sink thinking that maybe you would at least touch it for them.

Now don't get me wrong, there were some guys that I did see while I was out and pictured myself *ridin'* them all night. And, they hadn't even said a word to me or had even looked my way. Most men that are that attractive though, they didn't care. They were just like us women. They knew that their looks alone would make you want them as if they were the ones wearing the tight little dress and sunglasses. Although I wouldn't mind having a quick one-night stand with them, I just knew that it wouldn't be a good thing to have two drama queens running around in my apartment. Because if you even missed one of their calls or didn't text back quick enough, they would feel like the ones being used. Yeah, like us women always do. I would rather hear the *thug* say *fuck you then bitch* over the phone or through text when I didn't respond to them than to go back and forth with a man who thinks he was just God's gift to women. But, when you noticed that you hadn't been touched in months, you sort of began to feel like that loneliness was getting a little heavier by the day. So, the clothes began to get even tighter and the make-up became even more colorful and exotic. It was time to go out and act like a little hoe for a day or two.

Every once in awhile, I'll just joy ride someone to pleasure myself. But he had to be from out of town. Sometimes, and I hate to admit this, it was usually someone else's man. I felt safe doing this because I know they can't tell anyone about what we were doing. I wasn't in a relationship and I wasn't getting any dick so I thought it would be a great idea to just fuck around with someone I wouldn't have any ties to. We were both getting what we wanted from each other and then we just went separate ways after we were done. It got a little dangerous sometimes. Especially when his phone started going crazy as his woman called wondering where he was at. One day, I freaked the fuck out. He had told me that his wife had just left and was going out of town for the day and wanted me to come over to their house just to get a quick one in. I said ok, but I was shaking all the way there because I had never done that before. I wore a sundress with no panties just so that he didn't have to waste any time trying to unbutton my jeans or take off my shirt. I just wanted him to lick on me for a few seconds, get my pussy wet and just slide it in from the back.

As soon as he was getting ready to put the tip in, my heart just fuckin' stopped and my throat dried up. I heard someone knocking on the door. He was so into it that he just kept trying to slide his dick into my pussy. Men are fuckin' crazy. That quick nut sometimes just gets in the way of everything. They would lose their entire house and family trying to bust it. After the second knock, I quickly pushed him off and ran into one of the bedrooms. Stupid me. I should have just jumped right out of his kitchen window. So here I am now hiding in his master bedroom closet while he goes to answer the door. I could hear him talking, but I didn't know if it was his wife or a random person that had stopped by. After a few minutes, I hear the door shut and footsteps headed my way. I would have rather it been a warrant and that the police were taking me in as I heard the footsteps getting closer. All of a sudden, I see that the door opens and it's him with his rock-hard dick telling me to come out so we could finish what we had started.

Now I don't know about any of you other women out there, but I wasn't going to risk that a second time. I told him that I was too nervous now and that I just needed to go home. And you know how men are when they just want to fuck. They will not give up until they get it in. I got up, grabbed my keys and told him that I will meet up with him later on that night. But he didn't make it all that easy for me to just walked out. With my keys in hand and purse on my shoulder, I just spit in my hand, grabbed his dick and just started jerking him off. The faster I did it, the louder he moaned. The trick is to moan right along with him. Sometimes it felt better than fucking because you had all the control. And when I noticed that my hands were getting a little dry, I would spit in my other hand and continued until I finally saw his cum sliding down from the tip of his dick all the way down to his balls.

Unfortunately for them, these little adventures ended once I found a man to be with. I know, it's seems unfair to him. But he had a woman at home and all I wanted to do was to get fucked temporarily during my little dry spell. It was a dangerous game to play because I didn't want him to get caught and then feel like we were going to end up together. Because as we all know, there was always a chance that you would always lose them the exact same way that you found them. The same things he was doing to her were probably going to be the same things that he would have been doing to me. And that's not what I needed or wanted. I loved the little thrills of fucking him, but I knew that it wasn't love. There were no feelings involved although I could always sense his jealousy when he saw me speaking to other men in public. I sometimes did it purposely so that he knew that he did not own any part of me.

We suck as women sometimes. We call most men dogs, yet, here we are catching ourselves being little hoes sometimes. We do the same things that we wouldn't want other women to do to us. Then we have the nerve to say that there are no good men out there. Yes, it is very true when they say that most men just want to fuck. But what about us? We are no different. We want to fuck too. But when we can't find our own dick to fuck, we sometimes fall back and do things with another woman's man that we damn sure never want to be done to us. I guess you can say that most of us women do have a little hoe in us even though we would never want to be disrespected by being called one. I never wanted to lose control of myself between being bored and not having sex. Because that's exactly how you become known as a hoe and an easy fuck. Then, by the time you did find a good man, you prayed every day that he never heard about anything that you had done prior to you guys getting together. We always say that our past should never really matter, but it does. It can easily become a turn-off most of the time.

Spit

remember a friend of mine telling me that a man has already had sex mentally with a woman that they wanted way before they even said a word to them. I find that to be very true. Which it shows right from the beginning when they try to get with you. Unfortunately, we as women sometimes get so caught up with their words that we tend to forget that they really may just want to fuck. And that's where I have slipped at a few times. Some were really aggressive and would tell me what they would do to me if they were my man while others were cheesy as fuck when they would say stupid things like "bet your man won't treat you like I would". Which all that translated to me as "girl, I just want to fuck you". And they probably had a better chance coming at me that way and making me laugh than to listen to the same bullshit that other men have already said to me in the past.

But it was the smooth ones that would catch me off guard and get my attention. You know, like the strangers in the parking lot of a grocery store that saw me struggling with my groceries and offered to help me. Or the ones that just smiled as they walked by trying to say something to me and ended up nearly running into a pole. Because the less they said, the more curious I became. Especially if they were a little funny or just my type. Men need to understand that the quietest ones and the ones that says or does the least always has a better chance. It's when we are together that we want everything else to come out. It's a big turn off for us women to hear all of those nice things in the beginning that we know will eventually fade away once we let them in.

I am beautiful. Beautiful enough to know that I could fuck any man that I wanted to. But what does that really mean when I know that a man would fuck just about anybody? My beauty wouldn't matter to all men. I could be what a man wants, but would I be what he would need forever? Probably not. In fact, judging by the way my relationships have gone in the past it's clear to me that no matter how much of myself I have given to them, my appearance never really mattered. Funny how most of my ex's male friends would come around after we had broken up and try to get with me. I probably had a better shot with one of them than I did with the loser one that I had picked. But, rule number one, never fuck your ex's friend(s). Because it would be a matter of time before they would go around town telling everyone that you fucked the entire crew. And even when it is not all true, you will never be able to recover from that.

Most men brag about how big their dicks are. But here's my question. If their dick was worth bragging about, then how come they weren't at home pleasing the one woman that would want to fuck them every day? To me, size only mattered to a certain degree. It only mattered when it was someone that I was just fuckin' or if it was too small to the point where

I literally wasn't feeling any of it while I was riding it. Other than that, if I had neither one, I had no issues with watching porn and using my fingers to play with myself when I was feeling horny at home. But in the end, sex wasn't everything to me. As long as they had a great personality and just enough dick for me to ride and feel good even if it was just for a few minutes, I was ok with that.

Overall, I just wanted to be treated right. Because a man with a big dick thinks that everything is all about, well, his big dick. That was his answer to everything when we argued. "I could have any bitch I want". And let me guess why, "because you got a big dick". And when have you ever heard of a man with a big dick being loyal anyway. It always seemed like when hoes in the streets heard about his big dick that all of them just wanted to say they rode it. So, a big dick to me was better when I just wanted it for pleasure. Not to just have it at home as a trophy or it being used as a weapon to keep me trapped and in love.

Sometimes, I didn't even feel like having sex. Most of us women really need to understand that men don't just want to have sex all the time. I began realizing that when I would wake up every morning and walk around in my sexy brand-new Victoria Secret panties and a tight skimpy little tank-top and he wouldn't even compliment me or even try to fuck me from the back in the kitchen. As I walked by, I would stare into the mirror in front of me to see if he was even staring at my ass when I walked by. This motherfucker wouldn't even budge. I bet if I had done that the first night we had met that he would have probably took his dick out and fucked me on the kitchen table. But that's when I came up with the best idea ever on how to keep my man not only entertained, but also into me. You see, it doesn't take much to make a man happy. If a single NFL game or boxing match can get him all riled up for a few hours, imagine what a hand full of warm *spit* in my hand can do for him?

See, some of y'all women have this game all fucked up. You think that just because you have good pussy that a man is going to be satisfied and into you forever? The only dick that will stay loyal to you and never leave your side is that dildo or vibrator that you have tucked and hidden in your pantie drawer. I mean, has it ever crossed your mind that you just happen to be the lucky one to have ended up with the man with the "big dick" anyway? If he or it was that good, then how the hell out of all people did you end up being with him? And that's when I realized that dick size really wasn't everything. A big dick only really matters to lose chicks that barely had walls tight enough to even feel a normal size dick. So, here's the advice that I have for you women that will blow your mind.

You have to make him want your pussy. You can't just use it as a tool to keep him around. You have to catch him when he is into something that has all of his attention. Don't worry, he will never mind a little distraction. While he's sitting on the couch, go right in front of him and sit on the floor between his legs. If they are crossed in any way, don't say a word to him. Just sit on the floor, slide his legs open and sit there for a few minutes and act like you're into what he is watching. See, men don't think that we are ever into what they are watching, especially when it comes to sports. But we always have to somehow find a way to act like we want to get into it as well. Believe me, it works. They'll go back to their boys later on that day and be like, "you're not going to believe this shit" when you sit there and act like you really cared about who got knocked out or who scored that game winning touchdown. It works better at night, but it will be an even bigger surprise to them if you did it during the daytime.

After a few minutes, just start rubbing on his leg. Trust me, it doesn't take much, a man's dick begins to get hard as soon as touch him. Don't rub too fast or too rough, just do it gently. After a few rubs, you can bet that his dick will be rock hard. You can tell because he will adjust himself slowly and begin to sink his back deeper into the couch. When you feel that he is relaxed, slowly work your hand higher and then get comfortable enough to where you can feel his inner thighs. Once you make it there, he will forget what the hell he was watching. He wouldn't even care if his team lost or if the man he bet his entire check on on got knocked out. Because by the time you reach his dick, all he wants to do is cum as fast as he can so he can try to catch a little more of what he was watching. Once you have one hand on it, spit on your best hand and begin to slowly jerk his dick off. When you feel like you have him right where you want him, you can do so many things without trying to fuck. You can now play with your own pussy by using your free hand or you can just lick his dick after every ten or fifteen strokes. Ask him, *"does it feel good baby?"*

Don't suck it though. That's something that you should only do right before you both go to bed and are ready to go to sleep. Because sucking dick is no different than fucking them. After a while, it can bore them too. Men hate routines. You have to also be spontaneous. So, while your jerking his dick, make sure to remember to change speed every few minutes. Don't just go too fast where you want them to cum. Remember, your trying to please them, not just trying to make them cum. The funny thing is, remember when just a few minutes ago you had walked by them in your panties and they didn't even look at you? After a few strokes and them getting ready to cum, he'll be asking you to take your panties off so you can ride his dick. But don't do it. Jerk it a little faster and spit on it a few times while staring into his eyes. It will drive him insane. Once you hear him whispering over and over that he is *about to cum,* bring your head closer as if your about to lick and swallow it and then just stare at it from the side of his dick as it slowly rolls straight down off of the tip.

That's how you create a monster out of your man. Funny thing is that when you do this during the day, he will probably forget whatever plans he had. At least for the next few hours or so, he'll just be laying there tired as hell looking like he's the one that did all the work. Then, later on that night, all of that is going to replay in his head while he's in the shower, and you better be ready for it. Because there is a great chance that he is just going to want to fuck you like a rabbit when he comes out. And that's what you want. Fuck all of that lovemaking sensitive romantic shit. That shit only happens during the honeymoon stages. In fact, save that shit for your side pieces if you have one. Because after you've been together for a long time, none of that shit will really even matter.

At least a side chick or dude will appreciate it. My man would only get me flowers on my birthday or on Mother's Day. Other than that, when he did come home with flowers, it was only because he was trying to make up for some bullshit that we had disagreed or fought about. But that *spit* though, that's your secret weapon. But don't be stupid and only use it when you're on good terms. Use that shit when you're mad at each other too if you really want to fuck his head up.

Bad Choice

I always hated when a man's first words to me were, "hey, beautiful", especially when it came from strangers. Hey, beautiful to me began to sound more like "can we fuck" after hearing it for the millionth times. See, I'm from Brooklyn and in New York, you had to learn to ignore that shit because if you fell for every "hey beautiful" that you heard and let that get to your head, you would have turned into the easiest fuck in town. Because they were no longer approaching you based on you really being beautiful. They would constantly be on the lookout wishing that they saw you in public somewhere to approach you based on what they had already heard about you. Men talk. In fact, I've come to learn that men gossip more than women do. Don't believe me? Pillow talk with one of them about random shit in the middle of the night after fucking them and you'll see.

You'll probably end up with more than you ever asked for. Shit, as a matter of fact, you'll probably end up with enough information that will connect the dots to some of the stories you were trying to figure out. Because let me tell you, most men will do just about anything to get some ass. They'll do anything to get the pussy and they'll do even more just to keep getting it when it was good. Most of the men I have ever dated or "fucked", if you want me to make it clearer, where the type to show up late, call you from outside or blow the horn like they were picking you up in cab. Those were the types of assholes that I for some reason always attracted. They could have at least surprised me with roses at the door once in a while. But they were always the ones who acted like they wanted to spend a little "quality time" together and then somehow always tried to make it into my bedroom somehow. Before you knew it, there they were laying on my bed while continuing the conversation that they had started in the living room. Like, who the fuck asked you to come in here while I was getting dressed? It was always a clear indication that all they wanted to do was fuck.

So being that I loved the bar and club scene so much, I thought I had made the best choice for myself. By this time, I had turned down business owners, doctors, police officers, and even drug dealers who out of all of them, had the best *game*. But I've heard stories about them too. I've always heard that drug dealers were there to fuck you the best one minute and then end up in prison the next. Next thing you know, you find yourself not being able to go anywhere because they'll be calling you all day and all night every chance they could. The only great thing about being in a relationship with an inmate was that you knew they weren't out on the street fucking anyone else. I've heard that inmates would always have some of the best things to say when they were locked up. Even some of those letters they wrote made you want to stay loyal to them. They said everything that a free man couldn't think about saying even if I just threw my pussy at them. But, once they were free and back out on the streets, you barely ever saw them again. Now you're left wondering whatever happened to that ring that they had promised you or if that job they said they had lined up was even true. Years later, you then realize that you were the real inmate who was freeing their mind while they were incarcerated.

I wasn't trying to waste my time with an inmate though. That was just way too much work. All that traveling to go visit them three times a week and sending them money? That shit just wasn't for me. I needed a man that I can be with every day of the week. But as time went on and me getting older, I began to feel the pressure of not wanting to be alone forever. Not only that, I was beginning to feel like maybe this love shit just wasn't for me. I remember going back to my mirror and talking to myself wondering why I wasn't able to just find the right man that I could happily be with forever. Which leads me to a personal confession. There were times when I would just pull out my make-up box and get myself all fly and shit. My face looked just right and then I put on a brand-new outfit that still had the tags on them just in case I wanted to return it, right?

Then, I would take a few selfies in my mirror that always made me feel like the most beautiful woman in the world, then post them on Facebook and Instagram and write a caption that said, "Stepping out". Sad part about it though, once I saw that I got about a hundred likes and like twenty comments that I wouldn't even respond to, I would slowly begin to get undressed, wash off all of my makeup, take a quick shower and then just lay in my bed all night while everyone thought I was really out dancing the night away. I wasn't going anywhere. I just needed to feel pretty for a minute even though I didn't have a man to lay there next to me.

Here I was trying to fool the world like my life was *lit* only to just end up rolling over and hugging my pillow all night. Sad right? Well, at least I got over a hundred likes on my pictures. But even funnier and more entertaining than that were the early morning phone calls and random texts that I would get from my ex's for the next couple of days. Here I was on social media trying to find someone new to date and these fucking bozos just popped up out of nowhere as if they still had a say in my life. "Where were you at last night" or "who did you go out with"? First of all, mind your fucking business. And second, I don't have to explain shit to any of y'all. Why don't y'all just worry about them little bitches y'all was fuckin' while we were together, huh? And although I would act all pissed off about it, it just proved that they still wanted my pussy.

But, again, deep inside I felt miserable about not being in a steady relationship. It was almost embarrassing to be this beautiful and not have a man. I would go out to the mall or just ride around town all day and all I heard was "hey beautiful". It got really old after a while. They thought I was beautiful. My mirror told me I was beautiful. And my insecurities, well, they were fucking me all up. I mean, how the fuck is it that I can look and know that I was beautiful, yet, I had men walking up to me asking me why I didn't have a ring on my finger? That just did it for me. I wasn't wearing a ring because I didn't have a man and wasn't about to just put one on so that I could stop feeling stupid about not being married by now. In my thoughts, I could hear all these other bitches saying, *"that's what she gets for thinking she's all that anyway"*. So, I decided to just say the hell with it and started to fuck with one of the bouncers at the bar where I was a regular at.

The Bouncer

After a year of stressing about not being in a relationship, I was finally able to say that I had found someone new. It was a risk, but I thought that I had made the best choice out of all the men that had tried to get with me. I was tired of the "hey beautifuls" and all the rest of the dumb bullshit that men had been trying to say to me. It was time for me to just have a little fun and enjoy my weekends. It felt so good. I was on the dance floor with my friends while my man worked the door. Every once in a while, he would come inside and bring me a drink from the bar or would even take a quick break to dance a song or two with me. I no longer had to deal with all the desperate men who would offer me a drink or ask me to dance anymore. Now, I had all three. The drinks, the dancing and the dick. I felt as comfortable as I have ever felt when I went out. And not only was he good looking, he also had a little muscle to go along with it, which made me feel even more secure.

Our honeymoon stage was perfect. About three months into our relationship, I began to feel like he was really the one for me. I heard no rumors about him and there was no gossip being spread about us out there in the streets. He always answered my calls and responded to my text messages within five minutes or less. I never felt like he was cheating or using me in any kind of way. In fact, we saw each other almost every single day. We would take walks down by the pier or around town holding hands as if it didn't matter to him that anyone saw us together. That was rare in my hometown. You barely ever saw couples walking around holding hands or being out in public view. For some reason, it felt as though everyone was either cheating or creeping around somehow. Every time that I heard that someone had been caught cheating, it was always the ones you least expected. But since I was so happy with who I was with, that was no longer any of my business to be entertained by. I had to focus solely on my man and that was all.

Six months went by, eight months went by and still, it felt like the perfect relationship. The sex was great and so was his company. He dressed nicely and even kept up with his haircuts. He got an edge up almost every other day. I really liked that. He cared about his appearance. Sometimes I had to laugh because I didn't know who the biggest bitch was when I noticed that he would sometimes take longer than I would to get dressed and ready to go out. But, I'd rather that then the bums who had always tried getting with me. Appearance meant almost everything to me aside from a man's personality. If you were pretty good with those two things, then I wouldn't worry too much about the car they drove or how great their sex was. We could have always worked on those things. I just wanted someone next to me who looked good, smelled right and made me stand out when we walk anywhere together as one.

About 9 months into our relationship, I noticed that I had been drinking a lot more than I had ever before. I was coming home drunk almost three to four nights out of the week. I mean, he was a bouncer and I was getting drunk for free every night. So yeah, it felt great not having to spend any money while I was out, but now I was having a hard time getting up every morning to go to work. Before meeting my man, I was always on time for work. I was never late, and I had never been written up in the two years that I had been working as a dental hygienist. In fact, I only lived about fifteen minutes from my job. But fuckin with him and going out almost every day of the week almost ended up costing me my job. Suddenly, I was being written up for being late and for calling out sick too many times. Not to mention that I had already lost my part time job at *GoGetters* Auto Group where I was working as a part time receptionist because of all the partying that I was now doing.

As much as I wanted to be in a relationship, I had to really slow down a bit. I had to take a few steps back and remember that I also had bills to pay. I didn't want my relationship to be ruined by me slowing down on going out, but it was beginning to be a bit too much. I decided to invite my boyfriend over and have small talk about how I had been feeling. I didn't want to overdo it because I didn't want him to feel like I was ruining the great flow that we had since the day we met. This was the best relationship that I had been in since my husband and I divorced. I hated even thinking about that. I believe that I have been trying to escape those thoughts so bad that it landed me right where I am today. Ever since my ex-husband and I separated, I had fears of giving all of myself to a man. Being left by a man has always made me feel like I'm the one that failed. I barely ever blamed them and instead of just saying fuck it, I began to argue less and forgive more to avoid problems.

My ex-husband, unbeknownst to me, was an undercover junkie. He loved his cocaine. He never did it around me, but after about a year of being married, I began to see a big difference in the way that he was acting and the way that he was treating me. All I could do was pray to God and I even started going to church on Sunday's whenever I could to try and find the strength to get us through it. Nothing worked though. If you know anything about cocaine, you know that it involved a lot of partying and many females. And after a while, he started coming home later and later until one day, he just never came back.

He ended up leaving me for another woman that I assume he had been partying with the entire time that we were together. I say that because I remembered looking out the window about three months into our marriage and seeing him getting out of the same red car that he got out of the day that he came and got all of his belongings. The only strength that I felt God did give me was that day when I just sat on my sofa and watched him going in and out of our apartment as he took everything that belonged to him. Lord knows I wanted to go outside and drag that *bitch* out of her pretty little red BMW and beat the hell out of her. But what was that going to solve? It damn sure wasn't going to make him stay.

I didn't want to make matters worse by ending up getting arrested over a man that already had his mind made up to leave. So, I just cried about it for months until I was strong enough to just put it all behind me. Unfortunately, it was my daughter who had been suffering the most. It was so tough for me that my mother asked to take care of her in Connecticut because I was too unstable. My life was out of control. I just wanted to stay home and cry all day. I must have asked God a million times, "*why me*?" No matter how many times people tried to tell me that everything happened for a reason, I never wanted to believe that was he case.

But fast forward to where I am at today, I just didn't know how I was going to approach this situation with my boyfriend regarding how we needed to slow down with going out almost every night. Once he had come over to my apartment and made himself comfortable, I paused the show that we had been watching and asked him if we could have a quick conversation. This was probably our first serious conversation since we had met. By serious I mean that it just wasn't going to be one of those types of conversations where we were just going to end up laughing about it and moving on. Yeah, we've had small little disagreements in the time that we had been together, but nothing serious enough to where we had to stop talking for a few days or needed to take a break from each other.

Once he said, "sure, what's on your mind?" "Is everything ok, he asked?" I told him that everything was good but that I wanted to have just a quick conversation about how going out almost every night was beginning to take a toll on me out and causing me to lose focus of my priorities. He quickly interrupts me and says "Priorities?" As if to ask if our relationship was not a priority to me. I said, well "maybe I could have used a better word, "I'm sorry honey". Please don't be mad, I don't want this to become an argument, I said to him.

He says, "ok, go ahead, I didn't mean to interrupt". And that's what I loved about him. He was so easy going and really cared about my feelings. Not like every other man that I had been with that made everything all about them. I went on to finish telling him that we just needed to slow down a bit so that I wouldn't lose everything that I had worked so hard at maintaining since my divorce. In the end, he said that he understood and that he will definitely take my worries and concerns into consideration and that it was not going to change the way that he felt towards me.

I knew that going out was big for him because he always said that he enjoyed showing me off in public. He said that it also made him look good anytime that people saw him out with a *beautiful* woman. My confidence was at an all-time high because before I had met him, it was my mirror that would constantly remind me of how beautiful I was. Everything that I had done personally with any other man that I had messed around with seemed like it was just to pleasure them only to have me go right back home and crying into my pillow.

I decided that once we had come to an understanding about my new plans that I just didn't want to ruin the moment by just sitting around at home watching television all day. I told him that although I did tell him that I wanted to slow down with going out that it didn't have to start right away. I told him that since it was Wednesday, and I had the next day off that we could go out for a few drinks tonight since it wouldn't interfere with anything. The smile on his face made me feel better right away. He really enjoyed and loved being out in public with me. It made us both feel complete.

Which again was very rare because most of the men I knew were the type to want to come over at night just to get their little fucks in and go right back to whatever it was that they were doing in their personal lives. So, we went out to *Mambos* which was the name of the bar where he worked at. Only he was off that night which meant we were going to be drinking a hell of a lot more than we usually did. And, oh my God, from the moment we walked in, it was shot, after shot, after shot. I think we probably took down a whole bottle that night. I'm not sure if it was the liquor or my insecurities, but I swore that every chick that walked up in there was looking at us. I wasn't the jealous type, but I believe that I even caught one of them pointing our way. I didn't want to ruin our night out, so I just brought him in a little closer as we danced and ignored everything else that was going on.

We ended up dancing the night away and then went out to dinner right around the corner at *Thames Landing Oyster House* where a friend of his was co-owner and also the head chef at the restaurant. It was one of the best nights that we had ever spent together. Not only did we have a great time at the bar, I was also happy that he wasn't upset about our conversation back at the house earlier that day. It just felt perfect. There was just nothing that could have ruined our night. After sitting at the restaurant for a little over an hour, I noticed that it was getting a little late and that the crowd was slowly getting smaller by the minute. I asked the waitress for a to go box so that I could take my Shrimp Scampi home.

I was getting a little tired, so I told my boyfriend that I was ready to go home. He said "ok", got up and paid, shook hands with Jose, who was the chef there at the restaurant, and then we headed home. I didn't realize how *fucked up* I was from all the drinking until I sat down in the car. I told him that he needed to slow down because I didn't want to end up throwing up all over his front seat. The ride wasn't that long. I only lived a few minutes from the restaurant. And once we made it home, I noticed that he too was fucked up. I was so out of it that I didn't even notice that he had lit up a *blunt* while we were on our way home.

I was ok with him smoking his little weed here and there. It didn't really bother me. Especially knowing that it could had been worse. He could have been a cocaine junkie just like my ex-husband was. I mean, it's not like he was getting high all the time. But when we got home you can tell that he was still a little wired and wanted to continue on with the night. As soon as we walked in, we started kissing and feeling all over each other. I started to get in the mood although I was very drunk. I was so weak that I had to leave everything up to him on how he wanted to be pleased that night.

Up until this moment, I had never really sucked his dick. I had played with it, licked on it a bit, but we always ended up fucking soon after. Sucking dick was something that I barely ever did. I hadn't really been in a steady enough relationship and I wasn't just going to be sucking any man's dick just to satisfy them. Not because I didn't really like doing it, but I just didn't feel comfortable with doing that with just anybody. Especially if I wasn't in love and in a relationship where I knew he wasn't all mine. But that night, if I was going to be doing anything, that would have probably been my best choice. I was too weak to get on top to ride him being that I was so drunk, but I also didn't want to just lay there and be a *dead fuck* either.

We started in the living room and within a few minutes, we ended up in my bedroom. I remember taking his shirt off and kissing him all over his neck as I slowly worked my way down to his chest. Behind him, was my eight-foot mirror. You know, the one that always told me I was beautiful every day? So, I just knew that whatever was about to happen was going to be done right there on the floor, right in front of it. This was new to me. I was really nervous, but also curious to watch myself in the mirror as I was getting ready to please my man. The lower I got on his chest, the more relaxed he seemed. He began breathing a little deeper and whispering things that I could barely hear because his head was far back and facing the ceiling. I noticed that he then began taking his belt off and sliding his pants down. Such a typical man, he didn't even try to stop me even though he knew that I was so fucked up from all the drinking we did.

My mirror had never lied to me before and it had always made me feel better than any man ever had or ever could. I remember my thoughts trying to tell me to just go lay down and relax, but the liquor just kept telling me to just blow him and put him to sleep. Once he had his jeans and boxers down to about his knees, he then slid one leg up at a time and then took them all the way off. Good thing because I hated the thought of blowing a man while his jeans were all crunched up around their ankles while still having their shoes on. Not only did the thought seem *ghetto* as hell, it also painted a picture in my thoughts that once he was done *cumin'* that he was just going to pick them right back up, reach for his shirt and then walk right out the house.

Once his rock-hard dick was right there above my forehead, I remember starting off really slow. I began licking it and then jerking it slowly. Every few minutes or so, I would take a few seconds to look into my mirror only to see the thick drool dripping down from my chin. It wasn't a pretty site for me or what I thought it would have been like. The longer I stared in the mirror, the uglier I began to feel as I noticed my make-up running down the side of my face from the slow tears that were beginning to form in my eyes. It was the first time in my life that a mirror had ever told me I looked ugly. I felt that I had to hurry up and just get it over and done with. I didn't want to give him any reason to feel as if though I wasn't enjoying myself and upsetting him in any way. So, I kept my pace and even started to moan and jerking it a little faster just to make him cum quicker. I began to see and feel that his legs were beginning to shake, so I knew that he was very close.

The more I looked at my mirror, the uglier it made me feel. I tried just concentrating on the music that was softly playing in the background to distract me from feeling sorry for myself. We were listening to *Neyo*, who happens to be my all-time favorite. I had allowed my thoughts to sink into the song "Sexy Love" when suddenly, as he got closer to *cumin'*, I felt him put his hand behind my head while trying to shove his entire dick deeper down my throat. And as much as I wanted to please him, I just couldn't take it down that far. I was way too drunk and I felt like I was going to throw up after he made me gag a few times.

Like most men when they are ready to cum, all I heard was him repeating *"put it all in your mouth"* sounding as if he was getting ready to pass out. My jaw was starting to hurt and I was also beginning to feel dizzy. So, I made what I thought was a better choice at that moment. I slid my panties off while I still had his dick in my mouth and turned around to let him fuck me raw from behind. In a matter of a minute or two, he was done. I made sure he pulled out just in time. Once I saw him standing there behind me holding onto his cum in his left hand, I immediately went into the bathroom to pee thinking maybe I could get rid of any little cum that might have made its way inside of me. I grabbed a few wipies and handed them to him so he could clean his hands.

I then jumped in the shower to freshen up. I was hoping that maybe he would have jumped in with me. I showered for about fifteen minutes and when I came out, I notice that it was really silent. I couldn't even hear the music that he had playing from his IPhone anymore. I looked all over my apartment for him and he was nowhere to be found. I immediately put on my sweatpants and a t-shirt then went outside to see if maybe he was out there smoking the rest of his blunt or maybe just taking a breather. He was gone. I tried calling his phone a few times, but he never answered. I immediately felt like shit. I should have listened to my mirror. My heart felt like it had shattered inside of me. I tried calling him a few more times and it was now just going to his voicemail. *What the fuck?*

Disappearing Act

I had spent my entire day off crying on Thursday. Once I got home from work on Friday, I continued balling my eyes out to the point where I just fell asleep. I couldn't even eat. We hadn't talked or seen each other since he just disappeared from my apartment that night. We had never gone an entire day without talking or seeing each other since we met. Although I had already experienced what being heartbroken felt like in the past, this one pretty much destroyed me. I could still smell the scent of his cologne in my room as if he were still standing right there in front of me. I was left with so many questions. I even felt like I was going a little crazy in my thoughts because I began to feel as though my mirror had been trying to warn me all along. Every time I had to go in front of it, I felt as if I had to apologize to it like it was a real person with feelings. My reflection just didn't feel the same anymore. I didn't even feel like myself after that. I honestly felt like I was never going to be able to be in another relationship ever again. In fact, I felt like I just hated the thought of all men, period.

Early on that Saturday morning, I ran across a great idea. I didn't want to just sit around crying anymore. Although it had only been a few days, I began to think about all the men that I had dated, been in a relationship with, and even the ones that I just fucked around with and said to myself, "I am all done". I will never put myself through any more of this shit. If men thought that they were the only ones that could play those games, I was here to prove them wrong. I had been chasing after love for so many years and just when I thought I had found the right man to be with, I find out yet again that I was wrong. I didn't care if he called and begged for me to forgive him, *I was done.* I grabbed my phone and called my mother. After explaining to her about what had occurred, I waited for the right moment to ask her if she would be ok with me moving in with her in Connecticut. Without any hesitation, she quickly responded by saying "yes, I would love that". I immediately felt relieved.

As soon as I had hung up the phone with her, I called my job and gave them my two weeks-notice verbally over the phone. I didn't even want to wait until that Monday to give it to them in writing. I seriously wouldn't have cared if they told me not to bother with coming in anymore. I just wanted to be out of Brooklyn. God just happens to work in mysterious ways though. About twenty minutes after I had hung up with the supervisor, three of my girlfriends popped up to my apartment. They didn't even call to let me know that they were on their way, but I didn't care. I needed the company anyway. We sat around for hours just talking shit and the entire time, I didn't even think about my situation. In fact, it wasn't until one of them asked me if I wanted to go downtown and have a few drinks later that night that it all came back into my thoughts. For a second, I almost said no because I didn't know how I would have reacted had I run into my "boyfriend". I wouldn't want that situation to come up and then have it ruin our girl's night out. Not only that, I didn't want to second guess my plans of moving with my mother.

But you know what? I wasn't going to let that idiot fuck my entire weekend up and keep me from going out and having a great time. So, I told my friends that I would be ready by nine. They all said ok and then went home to get ready. These bitches must of have been feeling sorry for me without really saying it because they all came back to my apartment by seven-thirty with one bottle of Patron and two bottles of Candoni Moscato. Seeing all that liquor just reminded me of the last night I had been at the bar. The thought of how I felt that night almost made me not want to drink anymore. But, since we were going to be going out shortly, I picked the least strong one of the two choices and just drank some of the Moscato.

The Patron would have had me trying to give away my pussy to the first man I made eye contact with the way that I had been feeling. Let me tell you a little something about that Patron. If you're not at home drinking that shit, you might as well have gone out with no panties on. One night, that shit had me between an alley downtown with a dude that I had just met that same night. Had it not been because he didn't have a condom, I might have to honestly say that he would have *fucked* me right up against that brick wall. Yeah, I know, you just called me a hoe in your thoughts as soon as you read that, right? But ok, go look in your own mirror right now and act like you never had a one-night stand or left a man hard and walking away with blue balls shortly right after just meeting him. So, for me, Patron was definitely a big no-no.

Not to downplay the Moscato either, because that too can have you somewhere in the corner grindin' with a man whispering in your ear that he just wants to *put the tip in.* So, I had to be really careful about how much I drank before I went to the bar because I didn't want any man to feel like I was offering them my pussy if I smiled at them at the entrance. And speaking about the entrance door, guess who wasn't standing out there working? I started wondering if someone just came in my apartment and kidnapped him. Maybe the door was unlocked and someone who I used to fucked with walked right in and chased his ass out. I don't know what the hell could have happened. All I know is that I was feeling a little *tipsy* and I was about to go all in and have a blast with my friends.

We all walked in together, but all these *bitches* wanted to go straight to the bathroom and make sure that everything on them still looked good. Me, I didn't have that problem. I just knew that I was beautiful and that I didn't have to try all that hard. I didn't need to go straighten myself up for anybody. Especially when I wasn't even trying to be bothered by any of these drunk ass men. I didn't even care if I saw a glow around a man with a shirt that said heaven sent. Fuck all of them. I just wanted to shake my ass and talk shit all night with my friends, that was all.

As I waited for them to come out of the bathroom, I walked towards that back-end corner of the bar so I can pick a table that had a few chairs in case we just wanted to chill for the night. No sooner than me placing my ass on the chair, I turned around to see one of the lame ass bouncers standing right next to me. I thought he was going to tell me that I was sitting in the wrong section as if it were VIP or had already been taken. Before he could even get a word in, I rolled my eyes at him just to let him know that I was not interested in anything that he had to say to me.

I noticed my friends coming out of the bathroom, but they must have assumed that I was still near the entrance somewhere. Before I could even tell the bouncer that I didn't have the time to talk to him, he says to me, *"Yo shorty, I've seen you here a few times, you're the one that used to fuck with one of my co-workers, right*?" Judging by the way I looked at him he just knew that he had just pissed me off. I quickly became angry, but he looked like he wanted to tell me something about him. So, I responded with an attitude, *"Yes, what about him*?" He stood there for a second staring at me as if he was about to say something really important, but just didn't know how tell me. Before I could repeat myself to ask him again, *"what about him*?" He says, you know that he got arrested right? Confused, I said, *arrested*? He said, "yea, he was arrested late Wednesday night for grand larceny and for leading police on a high-speed chase".

I stood there repeating to myself over and over again, "what the fuck?" I asked him "how the fuck did he get arrested Wednesday night when he was with me at my apartment?" He says, "I called his phone to let him know that our boss had caught him on camera about five times going into the safe and stealing money and that the police had already been notified". He then said that all he heard "*my man*" say over the phone was "fuck that shit, I ain't going to jail" and that he then hung up.

Now that I think about it, he must of just ran out and took off in his car because he probably assumed the cops were going to come and get him at my apartment. I was just standing there mentally stuck. I didn't even know what to say. Even worse, I had already made plans to move to Connecticut with my mom because I was fed up with being played by all these men. I felt really bad, but what was I going to do? He was locked up and he hadn't even called me. It took for me to come down to the bar to find out that he had been in jail these past few days. I didn't know if I wanted to smack the bouncer for fucking my night up or just walk away in tears. I really felt like I just wanted to go home. I just looked at the bouncer and thanked him for letting me know then slowly began to walk towards my girlfriends. It felt like they were a mile away from me as I dragged my feet across the bar to meet up with them. Once I got to where they were at, I put my arms in the air and yelled "let's party *bitchessss*". Although my thoughts were all fucked up, I just put it all to the side for the time being.

Once we heard *Hypnotized* by Biggie come on, we all just ran straight to the dance floor. DJ *Breakdown* was on point that night. First Biggie, then Jay Z, right after that came Nas and then he just smoothed it all out by playing Old School R&B for like forty-five minutes straight. He was playing all of my favorite artists. He played 112, Keith Sweat, Mary J Blige, Usher, Beyonce', Faith Evans, Rhianna, and then out of nowhere, of all the songs the DJ could have played, "*Sexy Love*" by Neyo comes on. I ran straight to the bathroom as soon as I heard the beat and the first three words. By the time I had reached the bathroom door all I heard was "*My sexy love*". I screamed so loud as soon as I walked in. My friends had run right behind me confused about what I had just done. "What happened baby, one of the asked? I couldn't even talk about it.

Mary Jane'd

After ballin' my eyes out in the bathroom for about twenty minutes, we decided just to leave the bar and head back to my apartment. I couldn't believe that our girl's night was ruined that quickly. We weren't even there for an hour and now we were all just sitting around talking about what had occurred. They kept asking me if I was alright and if I wanted them to all spend the night so that I would not be alone. I told them that if they didn't mind staying, that would be great because it would at least help me get through the night. Once they decided to stay, we just began clowning around and it turned out to be one of the best nights I've had in a very long time. Most of us women seem to only think that a man or having some dick is sometimes the only thing that will make a night feel great, but not tonight.

It was a good thing that my downstairs neighbor was away on vacation because I know for sure that I would have heard the tip of his broom being banged up on his ceiling and through my living room floor. Or maybe not. We kind of had a *little something* for each other in the past. I used to let him lick my pussy every once in a while when I felt I was going through a little drought and needed to be *touched*. Every time I came home with a lot of groceries, he would be right there to help me bring them all upstairs. I fucked up one day and tried to be funny by saying, "Don't be looking at my ass while I walk up the steps either". We both laughed and he said, "Why do you think I always let you go up first?".

Oh my God, I was dying laughing. And then, when I thought about it, he was right, he was always behind me every time we went up. But I always thought it was because he didn't want to be rude and walk in to my apartment first. After that comment, he became really comfortable. Not disrespectfully, but he began saying little slick flirtatious comments like "why are you so *beautiful*, yet I never see you with a man?" And after the second time I heard him saying something like that to me, my dumbass one day replied, "well you better be careful because one of these lonely nights I'm going to end up knocking on your door". Stupid me.

The next time I came home with the groceries, he ended up *all in mine*. No, not those "groceries" either. I remember that I was wearing one of those sundresses, but it was a little shorter and tighter than the norm. Well, my ass just made it look a lot tighter. I guess it had turned him on so bad that when I walked into my kitchen, he was standing sideways because he didn't want me to notice that his rock hard dick print was going to show. Unfortunately for him though, he was wearing sweatpants and I had already noticed it, even before it got hard. In fact, because it had been a long time since I had been *touched*, I had bought him a six pack of Heineken Lights to thank him for all of his help. I knew those were his favorite kind because I would see his recycling bin almost filled to the top when he put them out on the curb. And if you thought he was already excited from looking at my ass as we walked the groceries upstairs, me buying him those Heineken's made him feel like I had always wanted to fuck him.

As soon as I told him that they were for him, he made one of those types of faces men make when they think you're trying to throw yourself at them and before you knew it, he was licking my pussy on the kitchen floor in front of my opened refrigerator. He licked me for so long the ice cream had turned into a milk shake in the trunk of my car. He did it so well that I actually did end up knocking on his door a few more times for him to come upstairs because I needed help putting a single screw in my wall or to help me move something heavy from one side of the room to the other. I was asking him to help me do shit I could have done all by myself but why not make it easier on myself and get something out of it, *right*?

Anyway, every time that he licked me, he always made sure that I would always cum. He was the only man that ever made me have an orgasm without even sticking his fingers or his dick inside of me. He was all tongue. Yes, of course he would rub on my clit a few times, but I would never just let him stick his fingers inside of me because that to me was more like fucking. And if that's what I wanted him to do than I would have just rode his dick right there on my kitchen floor. That's as far as he ever made it into my apartment. I didn't want him to get comfortable enough to feel like he was going to make it into my bedroom every time that he came upstairs. My neighbor really wasn't all that good looking so he wouldn't turn me on enough to the point where I wanted him to fuck me.

So, that went on for a few months until I finally ended up meeting *Jeron*. Oh, I'm sorry. I had never mentioned his name before because I was so used to just calling him my "boyfriend" all this time. I was a little hesitant about bringing him around when we first met because I didn't know how my neighbor would react. But when I finally did start bringing him around, I had to learn to play my position just right so that Jeron wouldn't become suspicious in any way. My neighbor was good with it. In fact, he played right along with it so perfectly that my boyfriend never once asked me why he had always been so friendly. He must have assumed that we were just great neighbors that got along really well. And being that he was not all that attractive, it made it easier for my man to never assume anything about us either.

The great thing about all of this though was that my neighbor also had a girlfriend. But she was hardly ever there. She had two jobs and he would tell me that she was always too tired to fuck him when she got home. I know, you just called me a *little hoe* again, but whatever. "Well, enough about my neighbor. I shouldn't have ever mentioned him to you guys anyways because I know that when you see him outside you're going to laugh at me due to him being so ugly", I said to my friends as I stood there with the blunt in my right hand finger tips.

Oh, where did I get the blunt from you might ask? Well, because I had spent a few days in a row crying on my living room couch, I never even notice that when Jeron ran out of my apartment that night that he had left an ounce of that *good shit* on my end table by my bed. One of my friends had just walked out of the shower and when she went to go turn on the lamp in my bedroom, she saw a blunt that had been halfway smoked and some more weed left in a sandwich bag. She came into living room walking straight towards me with the blunt in one hand and the bag in the other asking me why I had never told her that I smoked weed. I told her that I didn't smoke. She then asked, "Well, then what's this?". I said, "oh shit, *my man* must have left it here the night he ran out". Because I was already a little drunk from the Cardoni they had brought over, I didn't even hesitate to say, "*fuck it, light that shit up*". The last thing I remember was the flame from the lighter that had the letter J engraved on it and before you knew it, I was just rambling on and on about the stupidest shit that came to my thoughts. Such as the story about my big dick sweatpants wearing neighbor.

By the end of the night I had all these bitches on the floor. We stayed up till almost three in the morning telling stories. We ended up drinking all the liquor that they had brought over earlier that day. I felt bad for all of them because they were really trying to show me a good time, but the night was cut short due to my issues with Jeron. But they were the best. They all said that they understood and that they weren't even upset about having to leave the bar even though I still felt like shit over it. So, I figured that I would make it all up to them by trying to be a fucking comedian the entire night.

They each took turns taking showers and lucky for them, I always kept packs of new toothbrushes around because I just never knew who I was going to end up having to spend the night. I began explaining to them why I always had certain things available in my apartment. It was like having an emergency kit, but for sex purposes instead of for minor cuts and bruises. Having been single for so long, I always had to make sure that I even kept a box of condoms hidden in the closet just in case. It was always better to be safe than to be playing around and getting pregnant over a quickie. I learned that from some of the *players* I had always been used to dealing with. Anytime I stayed over their apartment, they always took care of me like I was at a hotel.

Only sometimes I had to check out a little early because some of them had little girlfriends that worked the midnight shift as a CNA or at fast food restaurants that stayed open later on the weekends. Now that I think about, it was probably those raggedy ass bitches who were stealing all the toothbrushes, wash rags and towels from their jobs and bringing them home. Because any time that I would ask for something to drink after we were all out of breath from fucking for those *three long minutes* that to him felt like forever, these ghetto ass cheatin' motherfuckers would always bring the cup wrapped around with a McDonald's napkin with a McDonald's straw in it. Shit, even when I asked them if they had salt and pepper, they would always tell me to grab it from the dining room table. And take a wild guess where those came from too? But who was I to judge? Even though all those towels were also being stolen from the convalescent homes, I was the one bringing my happy ass into all that *ghetto'ness* anyway, right?

Yeah, there was a time when I was out there being a little hoe. But guess what, this was my pussy and I could do whatever I wanted to do with it. In my thoughts I always felt like I was a classy hoe though. I was nothing like these dirty little bitches who thought throwing a little baby power and using baby wipes on their high mileage pussy after fucking was going to cover up the smell of fish bait. That was never me. I always tried to shower right before and I most definitely showered right after having sex. But you know what, whether they admit it or not, I do believe that it was safe to say that the majority of women do go through that little hoe'ish stage at one point or another in their lives. Especially if they hearts had been broken one too many times. Some just got stuck being one forever.

But being a hoe never really stopped any man from trying to get with them. Even after having about six baby daddy's and posting a hundred comments on social media talking about "*men ain't shit*", somehow someway there was always an out-of-towner who would come from out of nowhere and *wife'e* them up anyway. I couldn't believe how some of those men even ended up doing 25 to life over that ran down pussy for trying to kill someone over them. Here I was and I couldn't even find a man that would fuck me for 25 minutes and spend the rest of his life with me and those dudes were killing or dying over them dirty little hoes. Damn, wait a minute, how high am I right now? This was making more sense to me now than it did if I was sober. Anyway.

After that, I decided that whenever I needed an escape from reality, instead of just sitting around crying or complaining all day that I would just go and get zoned out by smoking some weed. I loved how I thought much clearer about of all these things that never seemed to come to mind when I was sober. I was so high and got into talking about fucking and sucking all night that somehow I ended up on top of my table in front of my friends and started performing *Freak Like Me* by Adina Howard. I stood up there pretending like I had a microphone in my hand and singing, *I want to pump-pump all through the night till the early morn.* I had never heard anyone laughing as hard as they were in my entire life. Once I was done being a clown and performing, I then had to try to figure out how the hell I was going to get my drunk and high ass off that table. The funniest thing was when they all joined in and started throwing dollar bills at me like I was on a stripper pole. Next thing I knew, I felt my entire body slide across my kitchen floor. They were all in tears after watching me trip and falling off my table.

Once I had picked myself up from landing on my chest, I moved on to the next topic about how some of these corny ass dudes were always coming up with all kinds of excuses to break up with women. I began explaining to them about a time when one of them broke up with me on my birthday because the dude that I was messing with was back home being nosey reading all the comments on Facebook and became jealous. Another one left me because I was almost on top of the bar screaming and arguing with the bartender because she thought it was a great idea to pour my fifteen-dollar Patron drink in a plastic cup. Like, "bitch, are you crazy?" But I believe that they were just tired and embarrassed from my behavior and did not want to fuck around with me anymore. I was a wreck at one point. It was then that I realized that most men don't really want to be around women that act all rowdy in public. And yes, I can admit that at times I was extra rowdy.

I understood why they felt like that too. I had become a little wild after my junkie husband left me. It seemed like I was always into something. But I've been trying to be a good woman and was really trying to learn how to behave myself. I'm always horny and in need of a little dick here and there, but I was at least trying not to throw myself around to just any man that walked past me. You know, like I said before, I was a *classy Red Bottom Stiletto wearing hoe.* And I always dressed to kill depending on the occasion and who the man of the week was at that time.

I always believed that there was a big difference between me and other women though. I was a little hoe and I can admit to that. The only difference was that some of them loved it a little bit too much and just didn't know when to slow down or stop. Like the stupid ones who would be letting different men drive their cars around town while they were at work. That alone was pretty much a dead give-away. It was really sad to see their cars go from being really nice and shiny to missing all four hubcaps with dents all over it. Even worse was when the doors and the hood of the car were an entirely different color from the original. A brand-new car and within six months you knew who it was coming down the street because we had the sounds that it made all memorized. Without even looking, I knew whose car it was by just hearing all the lose parts that were holding on for dear life by strands of duct tape. I was so high from telling all these stories that I didn't even realize what I was talking about until I heard all of them laughing and cracking up from all the stupid shit that I was saying.

Man, I was so high that my jokes just got funnier and funnier. I couldn't even take it anymore. I laughed so hard that I ended up with a headache. But at least it helped me forget about almost everything that had happened at the bar earlier that night. We got so caught up with drinking and laughing the night away that I never even had a chance to tell them about my decision to move to Connecticut. I figured that we had dealt with enough negativity already and I didn't want to ruin the rest of the night even more by telling them that I was going to be moving soon. So, I just thought that it was better to have waited for the next time we were all together again. We all just showered and finally went to sleep. But man, what a fuckin great night it was.

Charli

That Sunday morning for some reason we all got up early. We were all in the kitchen making breakfast by ten. Although we did get about seven hours of sleep, I didn't think that we would have all been waking up until later in the day based on how much we drank and smoked. I was so hung-over. They were still laughing at the crazy shit that I was saying and doing the night before. I was so fucked up that I barely remembered any of the stupid shit they were talking about. I was just happy that I was waking up to having them there though. It made my night a lot easier to deal with.

One of them mentioned something about me dancing on top of the table singing *Freak Like Me* and then landing on my face when I was trying to get down. But I knew that it had to have been true because I did have a little limp when I got up to walk from my bed and into the bathroom to pee and brush my teeth. While rinsing out my mouth in front of my mirror, out of nowhere came a thought of me wanting to get a tattoo. I've always wanted one, but I believe that the only reason why it came across my thoughts was because all my friends had one and I was the only one that didn't. Plus, I felt it would make me look and feel a little sexier. I didn't want to get a tramp stamp like the rest of the little hoes around town had. I wanted to get something different.

While scrambling the eggs, I turned to them and asked them if they knew of any good local tattoo artists nearby. All three of them had gone to the same person so they recommended me to go to him. None of them could go with me because they all had to go to work or already had other plans. So, they gave me the phone number and I called him later that afternoon to see if I could set up an appointment. He didn't answer the phone when I called him, so I just left him a voicemail. He called me back about five minutes later apologizing and telling me that he didn't answer because he didn't recognize the number.

He went on to tell me that they weren't open today because it was Sunday but asked me what it was that I wanted tattooed on my body. I told him that I wanted my nickname tattooed somewhere on my body but that I just wasn't sure where. He said, "I'll tell you what, if you're not doing anything around seven tonight, I can go and open up the shop just for you". I said, that would be perfect, I'll see you there at seven. I thought it was odd that he would have done that for me, but I didn't have any other plans and I really wanted to get my first tattoo done.

I was happy as hell that I had finally decided to go and get one done. I couldn't wait. Around six o'clock, I went and jumped in the shower so that I could start getting ready. The tattoo parlor was only about ten minutes away, so I didn't feel the need to rush. I felt comfortable with going down there by myself because my girlfriends knew him and they had told me that he was a really cool guy. Once I noticed that it was six-thirty, I sent him a text message to let him know that I was on my way and this time he quickly responded and said ok. When I made it down there, I had to knock really hard on the door because he was in there blasting his music. He finally came to open the door and we began by introducing ourselves to one another and he then led me to the station where he was going to be working at. He had a really nice set up. I browsed around the room and noticed the walls were filled with familiar paintings and photographs of events from *Cultured AF* and *Coco Dream* by Rosie. It put my mind at ease knowing that we had friends in common.

I saw him heading towards the back to grab his kit and the towels that I assumed were going to be used to wipe down the area of my body where I was going to be getting my tattoo done. Right then and there, once I started thinking about the needle and all the pain, I almost felt like I wanted to walk out. He was a pro, so he could tell just by looking at my face that I was nervous. He said, "relax *beautiful*, everything is going to be ok". There we go again with that word beautiful. But I didn't mind it coming from him. I understood that he was just trying to get me to feel comfortable. I noticed that he was wearing sweats, so I knew that there was a possibility that I was going to be able to see his print if I started flirting with him. I swear that these dudes with big dicks do that shit on purpose. I didn't mind it either. Sometimes it was exciting for me just to see their prints.

But I promised myself that I was going to be a good girl this time around. I do have to say though, he was fuckin' hot. He reminded me of David Beckham. He had tattoo sleeves on both of his arms, his muscles were just right and he had that five o'clock shadow on his face. On top of that, his hair was nicely combed to the side and when I finally took a good look into his eyes, it appeared he was already fucking me in his thoughts. All I kept telling myself was to concentrate on what I had gone there for and to just go home. Between his looks and us being there alone, I knew that it was going to be hard for me to just concentrate on getting me tattoo done. I almost felt like I was beginning to sweat just from the thought that he was going to soon be touching on my body.

I need a quick mental break. So, I asked him if he didn't mind if I stepped outside for a quick second because I had to make a really quick important phone call. He said, "ok", and I stood up and walked slowly towards the door while pulling my cell phone out of my Coach purse. I was walking slowly because I was trying to lower whatever price he already had in mind for the tattoo. I wanted him to look as I walked towards the door, so with my right hand, I slowly wiped at my ass only to bring his attention to it. As I made it closer to the door, the reflection in the window said it all. I stood there for a second while acting like I couldn't find the name of the person that I was trying to call, but I really just wanted to see if I had already turned him on. As I went to go reach for the door, from the reflection, I saw him reach into the front of his sweats to adjust his already rock-hard dick. I knew right from that moment that the price had to have gone down at least fifty dollars.

I opened up the door and made my way to the front and I called one of my girlfriends. It was actually the one who first recommended for me to call him. As soon as she answered the phone, I said, "*Bitch*, why the fuck am I here at the tattoo parlor about to get my tattoo and you never told me about how fine he was?" She just started laughing. She didn't even say a word. I just hung up on her and walked right back in. When I came back inside, I dropped my keys on the floor by "accident" but when I went to go pick them up, I actually turned my ass towards where he was sitting and reached down to pick them up. Once I turned around, I said to him "I apologize for that". He responded by quickly saying, "oh, don't even worry about it, not a big deal".

He must have thought that I was apologizing for going outside to make a phone call when I was really trying to apologize for bending over like that in front of him. I said, "no, I'm apologizing because I caught myself turning around to pick up my keys while having my ass all over your face like that". I explained to him that, "my shirt is kind of lose and I didn't just want to bend over frontward where he could look down my shirt". All he did was take a very obvious swallow of his own spit and smiled nervously. By then, I knew I had him. I thought that maybe I had worked it down to at least seventy-five dollars off whatever he was going to charge me.

After a few ideas and going back and forth, I decided that I was going to get my nickname *Charlie* tattooed on my right rib just under my tit. That would probably bring it down to about another hundred dollars off. I told him to go and put the blinds down before he started so that nobody would be able to look inside and by the time he came back, I was already laying on my back with one of my titties out. I mean, what did I care. I know he had seen many titties before and plus, I was moving out of state anyway. So, I said to him as he sat there in his chair right next to me that I wanted my nickname tattooed on my right rib and that maybe, depending on the pain, that I would think about adding a nice rose on my left rib. He said ok, but before he turned his tattoo machine on, I said in a soft sexy voice, *"please take it easy on me"*, as I placed my hand on his shoulder and slid it down to his bicep giving it a slow rub. I stared into his eyes for a quick second and then I just turned my head slowly away from him and closed my eyes.

He began to clean up the area around my rib in somewhat of a slow circular motion almost as if he was trying to be really careful about not touching my tit. I had firm tits, but they were big enough to get in the way of his hands while he worked the machine around. So, I told him that it wouldn't bother me if he felt the need do either have to move it a little or if his hand accidentally brushed up against it. As soon as I hear the machine going, I knew that I was about to be in pain. Once I felt the needle touched my skin, I looked at him and moaned while looking at him with a similar face like the one we make when we are about to have an orgasm, only I was in real pain.

After a while, I was numbed to the pain. By the time he got done with the R, he asked me if I wanted to take a quick break. I said "yes" because I really had to use the bathroom. I got up slowly due to my entire right side being sore and hurting a bit. When I came back from using the bathroom, I and asked him if he was ok we me just taking off my shirt because it was starting to be a little uncomfortable having to hold it up with my chin and also trying to keep my left tit in. The look on his face was priceless. He then asked, "are you serious?" I said, "yes I'm serious". He said, "whatever works for you works for me". Like I ever thought he was just going to say no. I took off my shirt and I immediately felt sexy with my tattoo although he wasn't done with it yet. All he had left were the letters *l.i.e* and I was already picturing myself at a Miami beach showing my shit off.

So here I was laying there with both of my titties out trying to work this price all the way down to damn near free. I knew that he was getting close to being done. And once I noticed that he was about to start working on the last letter, I asked him if we could take another break. Without any hesitation, he said ok, so I just laid there for a few seconds staring at the ceiling. I asked him if he had any water or something to drink because I was thirsty. He said that the only thing that he had to drink in the refrigerator was a little bit of orange juice then pointed while saying it at the same time, *"and that half of bottle of vodka over there"*. Once he said that, I knew what he was thinking. And I damn sure wasn't going to turn it down.

I had heard somewhere that you shouldn't really drink alcohol before or while getting a tattoo because it would thin out your blood and that it would just make a big mess. But at the same time, I have also heard about people who do it while they are entirely *shit-faced* too. So, I asked him if it was ok for me to have a few shots of the vodka since he only had one letter left to do? He sort of scratched his forehead really quick and without even answering me, he got up and just poured some of it in cup for me. I felt as if he knew that I was trying to *play* him. But at the same time, a part of me also knew that he would probably wouldn't mind *fucking* me too.

After back to back shots, I asked him for one more before I laid back down. He just looked at me as if I gave him the impression that I was going to end up drinking the rest of the bottle. I told him that it would help me out a little with the pain and before I could think of another bullshit reason for one more shot, I happened to look to my left really quick. I noticed that they had a really long mirror on the opposite side of the room that I didn't see when I had first come in. I got back up and slowly made my way towards it. As I stood there in front of it with my brand-new tattoo and my titties hanging out, I asked him to come over and stand behind me. Again, without hesitating, he stood up from his chair and walked towards me. I didn't want to turn around all the way because I didn't want to make him feel uncomfortable if I made it obvious to see that his dick was hard even though I had already noticed it earlier when I walked back in.

I was wearing my favorite jeans that day and my brand-new pink and white Lebron's. They made me feel and look a little *"tom boyish"*, but at the same time also made me feel cute and sexy. Especially with my new almost finished tattoo. As he got closer, I asked him to stand behind me and put both of his hands on my tits and hold me tight for a few seconds. I know that he was totally confused by what I was asking him to do. He didn't disappoint me either. Once I felt both of his hands over both of my fully erected nipples, I pulled him closer towards my body so that I could feel his dick up against my ass. Suddenly, I began to feel his lips kissing me softly on the back of my neck and then on my right shoulder. I was ready to fuck him right then and there. Those shots I had taken made me feel buzzed.

There was a fan right above us so the air coming down was giving me goosebumps every time he licked on me. I told him to stop for a quick second and asked him if he had a blanket long enough to be able to cover up the mirror. He said he did have one, so we went and grabbed it from one of the rooms in the back. I wasn't trying to waste any time. I noticed that he was taking a little longer than I expected to come back with the blanket, so I went and grabbed the bottle of vodka and quickly took down another three shots. When he finally did make it back, he actually caught me with the bottle in my hand. He said, "go ahead, take another shot if you want to". I said "ok" and took down one more shot before I started making my way back towards him. I asked him to please cover up the mirror first and then since it was obvious that I was going to be ridin' his big dick, I asked him to take his sweatpants off and go sit on the couch. I stared at him for a few seconds as he pulled them down and once they were completely off, I then asked him to slowly begin jerking his dick while I watched. That shit was humongous. I could have used both of my hands to hold it and there was still enough room for a third hand to help me jerk it.

I knew that it was big just based on where the tip print was at when I first saw the reflection in the window when I had arrived. While he played with his dick, I licked my fingers and began to slowly rub on my pussy while sticking two of my fingers in my pussy just to stretch it out a little before he put the tip of his head in. I knew that I was already in pain from the tattoo, but I also knew that I was going to have to prep myself for him to fuck me too. His dick was twice the size of any man I had ever slept with before. Once I saw that he was giving me that look and biting his bottom lip, I leaned down and basically drooled a mouth full of spit on his dick so that I could lubricate it as much as I could and sucked on it for a bit before I put it in my pussy. I took a big risk of fuckin' him without a condom, but I had got so caught up in the moment that I didn't want to ruin it by asking him if he had one.

I had been riding him now for about twenty minutes before he stood up and just began fuckin' me standing straight up. It was so long that he did it all in one motion without it slipping out. Once he began to lose his breath, he turned my ass around and just began trying to shove his entire dick inside my pussy from behind. I was seeing stars, but it was feeling so damn good. I felt it everywhere. It felt as if it was all the way up my stomach. I began rubbin' on my clit and moaning louder and louder until I felt his legs shaking and all of a sudden, I felt his warm cum shooting all over my lower back as he rubbed the last bit on my ass from the tip of his dick. I was in heaven. I didn't even have the energy to stand back up.

After about three minutes, I stood up to go clean my pussy in the bathroom sink. I immediately felt like he had stretched it out like it had never been stretched before. It was the best dick I ever had inside of me. It was crazy because he could only put half of it in me or else I would have literally been in stitches. I had to laugh at myself because I knew that he must have heard my pussy fart as I turned around to away from him. When I got to the bathroom, I noticed that the soap was a little wet. I figured out why he had taken a little longer to go and get the blanket.

He must have been in the bathroom washing his dick because I had smelled the same scent from when I had my entire face between his nicely shaved *horse dick* and kiwi sized balls. I caught myself staring into the mirror smiling because he made me feel like I have never felt before. He made me cum three times before he did. What I loved the most was that he was quiet almost the entire time except when I had sucked a little harder on the tip of his dick before we started to fuck. Men love it when you lick around the tip. It's a lot similar to how we feel when they feel or lick around our clit.

He wasn't one of those types of men who would use their dicks to punish you just to make you scream and see how many different faces you would make. He was just right. At one point, I felt like a thoroughbred horse at the Kentucky Derby by the way he grabbed my hair from behind and began to sound like he was getting closer to the finish line. When we were going slow, it felt like I was laying down peacefully and alone on the white sands of an island beach while listening to the sounds of small waves. But when I turned around and wanted him to just tear me the fuck up from the back, he grabbed both of my wrists and placed them on my back like I was being handcuffed. I was making so many different sounds that if you would have heard me from outside, it would have sounded like you were at the zoo walking by a hundred monkeys and caged up birds.

After getting all my shit together, I walked up to him and told him that I had an amazing time but that I was ready to go home. He said, "wait a minute, what about the last letter of your name on the tattoo?" I said, "you know what, I actually love it even more the way that it is spelled". It was different to me. Plus, it will always remind me of why we never finished it. So, I decided to leave it spelled that way. But before I walked out, I asked him, "How much for the tattoo?" He smiled, and said *"Charli, you can come back next Sunday and get the last letter and another tattoo for free if you wanted to"*. I smiled, gave him a hug and a kiss on the cheek then started to make my way towards the door. When I reached into my purse to grab my car keys, I noticed that I had three missed calls from a number that I did not recognize and a voicemail. I immediately unlocked my phone and listened to the message. It was Jeron's mother.

In the quick message that she had left on my voicemail, it sounded like she was crying. She began by telling me that her son wanted me to know that he was sorry about what had occurred the last time we were together at my apartment. She then explained that he wanted me to know that the reason why he had not called since he had been arrested was because he was thrown in solitary confinement for punching another inmate in the face who had been *accusing* him of an incident that had occurred many years ago. She never mentioned anything regarding what the incident was about. Before reaching the end of the message, she told me that she would try to call me once she heard from him again and that he also wanted me to know that he really misses me and that he *loved me.* Once again, I felt mentally stuck.

Beautifully Cursed

I felt like shit when I got home. One minute I was on cloud nine and the next I was back at home crying hysterically into my pillow. I began to feel like I was the unluckiest person on earth. I had been trying to do everything to just move on and do things to distract me from all that I had been going through but it all just continued to haunt me. I felt overwhelmed. My head just felt heavy. I had tried to go out to the bar and have a good time with my girls and the bouncer fucked my night up. Then I go get a tattoo to make me feel better and ended up having the most amazing sex that I *ever* had. But nothing seemed to help me get away from my situation with Jeron.

And I know what you are thinking. This situation with Jeron only occurred just a few days ago, right? But understand this. I have been through so much that no matter how hard I tried or how much I did to be in a happy relationship, something always occurred where I would end up hurt or heartbroken. I felt like I was constantly being punished. Even the side chicks around town were having better relationships and seemed happier than I was. The more I thought about it, the more I couldn't wait to leave New York. Although going to live with my mother would sort of have me feeling like it was a set-back, I needed change.

I began to feel like no matter what I tried to do to find happiness that it just wasn't meant to be. I felt like I have lost all control. Not only was I losing control of myself mentally, I was even beginning to lose track of how many men I had fucked since my divorce from my husband. Off the top of my head and by counting backwards starting with the tattoo artist, I counted eight of them. The longer I sat there in front of my mirror crying the more I began to hate myself. I even began to yell at my mirror and blamed it for always lying to me by telling me that I was beautiful as the list of men grew longer in my thoughts of the ones that I had *fucked*. All of a sudden, right in the middle of yelling "fuck you", I threw my metal framed make-up box straight through the middle of my mirror and once all the pieces of the shattered glass hit the floor, I just stood there in complete silence.

As the time went by, I began to slowly feel myself becoming more relieved. I didn't even feel mad at myself for breaking my mirror as I began to sweep up all the glass from my bedroom floor. Once I was done, I found myself on my elbows and knees on the kitchen floor and praying for God to give me the strength. It felt so peaceful. The last time that I had remembered praying was when my ex-husband and I were having problems towards the end of our marriage. It never once came to mind that while as I was praying for God to save us from having to go through a divorce that maybe he was just trying to open up my eyes to realize that he just wasn't going to be the man that I would be spending the rest of my life with. It was at that moment that I decided to just pray every morning and every night for God to just take over and guide me. I was tired of feeling like I was going to somehow fix or change all of the outcomes or even have total control of everything that was occurring in my life.

From one day to the next, I began to feel a lot lighter on my feet. I no longer felt the need to waste hours in front of a mirror or even put on make-up to try and look better. Instead of relying on mirrors to tell me that I was beautiful, I slowly began to feel it more in my heart and it became less about my face and appearance. The more I began to feel this way, the more I felt like I had it wrong all along. Those men didn't want me, they wanted my body just to brag to each other and say that they all had me. But you know what? God had a strange way to make all of those things feel like they occurred a thousand years ago. And that gave me all the strength that I needed to better myself to move forward.

By this time, I had already called my mother and told her that I was going to have to temporarily cancel my plans of moving to Connecticut with her. I even walked into my job and went straight to my supervisor to let him know that I had changed my mind and was not going to be moving out of state anymore. They were really happy about my decision to stay because they really loved me there. I felt bad about telling my mother that I was going to stay in Brooklyn a little longer. Luckily, my mom had never told my daughter that I was going to be moving in with them. Although, I had changed my mind at that point, I still continued to visit them every chance I could on my days off from work. I just had too much going on and didn't want to make that move without fixing all of drama in my life and then ending up right back in Brooklyn trying to resolve them. And it truly didn't make feel like I was making a big mistake by staying because after praying about it for so many days, I felt like God was now in control of my life. I was at total peace with my decision. All that I wanted for myself was to be a better mom and role model to my now four-year old daughter.

Funny how most of my great ideas always came in my kitchen though. While I stood there waiting for the water to boil, I came across yet another great idea. Only this time, I didn't have to worry about anything crazy happening to me all over again. I decided to do what most women do when they want to get back to feeling pretty again. You notice I didn't say beautiful, right? Having been called beautiful almost every day by so many different men, I just began to hate that word more and more. I decided that I wanted to cut my hair into an entirely different hairstyle. I've always had long straight hair. And for years, thoughts of wanting to cut it shorter came and went. But now I was ready for a different look.

I went and checked my schedule to see when my days off were. As I am looking, I could hear my phone vibrating into my ringtone. It was Jeron's mother calling again. I had been wondering why so many days had passed since the night she had first tried calling me while I was getting my tattoo. After being on the phone with her and noticing that I didn't hear his voice, so I just figured that she was just going to be relaying another message from him. But then she says, "hey, would you mind coming over around four-thirty, Jeron wanted you to be here when he called?". I said "ok, I'll be there at four just in case he calls earlier". She said "ok" and then we hung up.

I remembered praying at my apartment before I left to go to her house. All I asked God for was to take and have total control of everything that was happening in my life and to remove anything that was going to get in the way of the path that I felt he was trying to create for me. I then grabbed my keys and my sunglasses from the table and made my way to Jeron's mothers house. I felt a little uncomfortable once I got there because I had never met or had spoken to her before. I knocked on her door and immediately, she just dove right in. About twenty minutes into our conversation, she had started to tell me almost everything about her son's past and how this was not the first time that he had been locked up. Right after making that comment, the phone rang. It was Jeron.

Red Flags

After talking to Jeron on the phone for about twenty-five minutes, I made sure that I saved a few minutes for him to be able to talk to his mother. When she heard me trying to tell him that I was about to put his mother on the phone, I noticed that she had been trying to waive at me to tell me that she didn't want to talk to him. I was so confused by that. So, I just continued talking until the recording between our voices reminded us that we only had one-minute left on our phone call. One thing that I did almost forget to ask him about was why it had taken him several days to call from the last time that he wanted his mother to relay the messages to me. He said something like, "You know how it is in here", and before I could even say "No, I don't know how it is in there", the phone call ended.

I didn't know if that was a hint from God trying to tell me that his reason was about to be all bullshit or that maybe he just had something else to hide from me. Once our call ended, his mother made her way back to the living room from the kitchen and asked me if I was ok. I told her that I was and then she asked me if I was hungry as if she just didn't want me to leave right away. I told her that I had just ate at home and wasn't hungry. She said "alright" and then I noticed that she sat down across from me and just started *going in*. I learned more about Jeron in one hour talking with her than I ever did the entire year that we had been together.

The stories that I had heard about him just did not fit the description of the man that I had fallen for. And you know what they always say, moms always know best. She told me everything about her son as if she was trying to warn me herself about being with him and told me to be really careful with anything that I ever did for or with him. You can tell that there was something more important that she wanted to tell me about him, but it seemed like she just wanted to *dance* around it until she felt comfortable enough to tell me. She asked me, *"Have you ever noticed those scars on his forehead and on his chin?'*

But before I could even say "yes", she said, "never mind that for now" and just moved on from the subject. We spoke for about another hour or so and after I had caught myself yawning a few times, I told her that I was feeling a little tired and needed to go home to get some rest. Finally, we said good-bye to each other as she walked me to the door. Once I was in my car, I had to turn back around because there were a few things that Jeron had told me to ask his mother about but because I was so deep into the conversation with his mother, I had totally forgotten all about it.

I made my way back to the door and rang the doorbell. When she answered the door, I told her that while I was on the phone with Jeron, that he had given me the phone number of a lawyer that he wanted me to call, but that I needed the money that was *stashed* in his closet in order for me to be able to pay for his case. She went into his room and came right back with a Nike shoebox. Once she took the top off, I noticed that it had about six different stacks of money all wrapped in different color rubber bands.

As soon as I saw the way the money was kept, I immediately thought one of two things. Jeron was either a drug dealer and I didn't know about it or that it was the money that he had been accused of stealing from the bar where he had been working at. Either way, he told me that all I needed to pay the lawyer was three thousand dollars and to just save the rest for an emergency. And that first emergency came very quickly. I was going to be using a few of those dollars to pay for my new haircut the next day. There were a few other "emergencies" that I found myself digging in the shoe box for soon after that too. All I had to do was make sure that the lawyer was paid in full first before I had my little fun with it myself. I said thank you to his mother and walked right back towards my car.

Before driving off, I sat in my car looking up the phone number to Glamatixs Hair Salon where my friends and I used to always go to when we really wanted to look our best. I called the salon to make an appointment and after being put on hold for about a minute, I was finally able to get through. My friend Ashleigh came to the phone and asked me if tomorrow at one was ok? I told her that one pm was perfect because I had a few other things that I had to do earlier that day. I was very happy that I was able to make my appointment with her. I didn't really trust anyone else with doing my hair. She was the most well-known hairstylist and make-up artist in the area and plus her salon had been rated the best in the area for the past five years. After making my appointment and hanging up with her, I just went home and tried to unwind.

Reality Check

woke up the next morning and immediately thought about the plans that I had for the day. Ever since the moment when I threw my make-up box through my mirror, I always remembered the one thing that I learned and needed to do from that day on. I knew that before I would get my day started that I always had to first pray and thank God for everything that he had done for me. I never asked him for anything other than to just be by my side and to help me if he ever saw that I was about to make the wrong decisions. I no longer cared nor was it a priority for me to jump on social media to see how many likes or how many comments I had before I spoke to him first. I needed real change in my life. It became a habit for me to pray first thing in the morning and it would also be the very last thing that I would do every night.

Praying always made me feel relieved. It even helped me to deal with my problems a lot better than the way that I had been used to dealing with them. Anytime that I felt like I was having difficulty with anything or anyone, I would go and find a quiet place and close my eyes to pray for God help me get me through it. The more I began to get used to praying, the more I began to feel like he was the only answer. And today was the day that I was about to find out that God had been trying to get my attention to let me know that he was trying to warn me all along from day one.

That morning, after finishing my breakfast and getting dressed, I went and called the lawyer's office and asked for the person that Jeron wanted me to go meet with. Luckily, I caught the lawyer just in time as he told me that he was about to head out to get something to eat at Dunkin Donuts which was right across the street. He told me that he was free for the most part and that if I wanted to start making my way towards the office now that he would be back by the time I made it there. I said "ok" and told him that I would be on my way. When we hung up, for some reason or another, I began to feel a little like my old self. I guess that the reason why I felt that way was because anytime that I had ever told a man that I was on my way was for all the wrong reasons and something crazy always ended up happening.

So, I knew that I had to be really careful about the way I presented myself when I arrived at the office. While I was parking my car, I noticed that there was a man standing in the front of the building looking to his right and then looking to his left until he saw me in the parking lot and then began walking towards my way. It was a private parking lot for lawyers only, so I thought that he was coming to tell me that I couldn't park there and that I had to move. I pretended to be looking for something around my car to play it off and when I looked back up, he tapped softly on my window. I couldn't really see his face because the sun was directly behind him and it was going right into my eyes. I rolled my window down a bit and I heard him ask, "can I help you?" I said "yes" I am here to meet with a lawyer that

I had just talk to a few minutes ago and told him that I was on my way.

"Oh, yes, that was me who you spoke to". Next thing I knew, he was opening the door for me and extended his arm out as if he was trying to help me with getting out of the car. By that alone, I knew he was raised right. But, like I said, I was there for business and business only. I didn't want to offend him either, so I reached over and allowed him to help me get out of my car. It was kind of nippy outside, so he told me to just hurry up and follow him in to the office. While walking in with him, I noticed that he had not let go of my hand from when he assisted me with getting out of my car. In fact, he held my hand all the way until he had to reach for his keys to open the front door to the office.

For a moment, I had lost all my concentration. Not only because he had held my hand for that long, but because I had just met him and within two minutes, he had already done three things that I had barely ever experienced any man do for me before. Not to mention the fact that it was all coming from one man at the same time. First, he was patiently waiting for me outside in the cold, then, he came over to my car and asked me if I needed any assistance. For him to open my door to help me was what really caught most of my attention. I've dealt with so many assholes that didn't even open my door for me to get into the car, never mind helping me get out of it. Even more impressive, not a single "hey beautiful", "damn girl you look so good" comments, or even the most typical, "do you have a man" questions.

Once we made it into his office, I couldn't help but notice how clean it was and how the scent coming from the candles on his desk just took over the entire room. The scent reminded me of the candles that I had just bought from my friend Betty at Striking Tela. And not only did all of those things catch me off guard, only to make matters even more uncomfortable for me, he looked like he could have been mistaken for Idris Elba. I'm sorry that I have to say this, but for about ten minutes, I had forgotten why I was even there in the first place. There was even a split second where he was trying to tell me something and all I saw were his lips moving. I had to quickly snap out of it. I interrupted him and asked him where the bathroom was so I could go and gather my thoughts. At the rate that my mind and my heart were racing, I had to ask him to please excuse me for a few minutes. He said, "yea, go right into the hallway and you'll see it right there on your left". I really needed to take a minute and go somewhere to pray.

Of course, I didn't really have to use the bathroom for any other reason other than clear my mind and focus on what I had come there for. I had to pray to God so that he would help me control myself and to also give me a hint about this man and the situation that I was currently facing. Because the way that I felt after being there for just ten minutes was beginning to feel like he had really been heaven sent. I know exactly what you're thinking as you sit there and read this too. You're probably saying to yourself, "here we go again". And trust me, I do understand why you would feel that way. I have given you many reasons to think that I was never going to change. Only one thing was different about me this time. I no longer cared about what anyone thought or felt towards me. Because if there is one thing that I have learned since I started to put everything in Gods hands was that, He, was the only one that could judge me. But *Mr. Idris*, well he was definitely the best looking man I have ever seen in person.

After praying for a few minutes, I made my way back to the office to finally talk about Jeron's case. I began by telling him that I had no idea about how the system worked or how to even go about fighting a case. He said, "don't worry about it, that's what I am here for". Before we went any further, I apologized to him and told him that I had totally forgotten to introduce myself to him by name. He then says, "Charli, right?" I asked, how did you know that? He said, "because you introduced yourself to me as soon as you had walked in, you don't you remember?" I must have been so deep in thought about his looks that I couldn't even remember if he had introduced himself to me by his name. Instead of asking him what it was, I just leaned in and grabbed one of his business cards. He said to me, once he noticed that I had grabbed one, that I didn't have to call him Mr. or even by his first name. He said, "you can just call me "E" for short. I said *ok E* and thought nothing of it at the time.

He then asked, "so, how can I help you today Ms. Charli?" Oh my God, even the way he just called me "Ms. Charli" had me going crazy inside. It sounded like he was trying to flirt a little, but it might have just been me wishing that he was. Thank God I had already put all of this in his hands when I went to the bathroom. But I honestly felt like anything that happened from that point on was what God wanted to occur. So, I started by answering his question. I told him that I was there to drop off three thousand dollars for a *"friend"* of mine to go towards his case. "Ok, what's your *"friend's"* name, he asked?" I told him that his name was Jeron and as soon as I said it, he said, "ohhh, good ol' Jeron". As soon as I heard the way he said that, I didn't even bother with asking him why. He probably already knew about some of the same things that his mother had told me about which made me feel like I must have been the only person who was totally unaware of and blind to.

After about an hour and a half, I had given him all the information that I felt he needed to know and then handed him the money. He didn't even bother to count it. He just took the envelope and put it in the drawer to his right. When I looked up to say, "thank you", I noticed that he was just sitting there quietly with his hands interlocked through every finger and his elbows on his desk. It appeared like he wanted to ask me something but just didn't know if he should or not. So, I went on to say finally say thank you for his time and that it was a pleasure meeting with him. He said, "you're welcome and the *pleasure* was all mine, but I have a question for you if you don't mind. I said, *"No"* I don't mind, what's the question". Never in a million years did I ever think that this man would ask me this question.

Made me even wonder if he had paid any attention to anything that we had just talked about or if he was even going to bother with taking on Jeron's case. I mean, he didn't even care to count the money that I had given to him. This man, stands up from his desk and asks me, "do you believe in God?" I answered him quickly without even thinking about it, *"absolutely"*. He then asked, "are you in a relationship now or are you single?" Before I could even answer the question, he says again, "I hope that you don't mind me asking you that question, but I just happen to wondering why a woman such as yourself would be dealing with a man like Jeron?" I was left speechless. I didn't want to ruin the moment. So, I just simply opened the door, but before walking all the way out, I turned around out with a big innocent looking smile on my face and said, "have a good rest of the day and hope to hear again from *really* you soon".

Revelations

*I*t was almost one o'clock and I didn't want to be late for my hair appointment with Ashleigh. After having that meeting with "E", I started to have mixed feelings about being too involved with Jeron's case. Between everything that his mom said about him and the way that "E" looked at me when he found out that I even knew him made me realize that he was definitely not the man that God had picked out for me. During our conversation, "E" had mentioned that Jeron was probably looking at a five-year prison sentence which did not sit well with me. Not only was I not planning on having to support a man in prison, I wasn't just going to be sitting around waiting for him to get out either. I know what you're probably thinking. You're thinking that I am being disloyal. But please come back and tell me if you still feel that same way in just a few minutes.

I finally made it to Glamatixs. I was about ten minutes early and Ashleigh was running a little behind schedule. But I was ok with it because I didn't have anything else to do after my appointment. And where better to be at than to be surrounded by a bunch of gossiping women, right? While looking for a place to sit, I heard a man's voice yelling out my name like they were really excited to see me. For a second, I didn't even want to turn around. With the problems that I had been dealing with the past couple of weeks, I didn't want to bother with another man trying to come over and even talk to me. I pretended like I didn't hear him and just sat down then quickly pulled out my phone just to play it off like I was answering a text.

"Chaaaarliiii", I hear my name yet again and I felt like I had no other choice but to look up because this time it had sounded like he was a lot closer to me than he was when he had first yelled out my name. When I saw who it was, I stood up so fast and ran all the way up to him and jumped right into his arms. It was my cousin *Franc Grams* who I hadn't seen in forever. We would always text each other but he always seemed like he was busy doing something. If he wasn't making music, he was out promoting talent shows or buying water guns for hundreds of kids around town to have water wars during the summer.

He was just always into something. We both sat down and just started catching up. I loved talking to him because he was always just so animated when he told his stories. I needed that energy too. By the time I had finished talking to him, I felt like a brand-new person all over again. But, because I was his little cousin, he didn't leave without telling me that he too thought it was a bad idea for me to be messing around with a man like Jeron. He gave me a big hug and told me that he would call me later because he had to get back to selling tickets for his upcoming talent show at the Garde Arts Theatre. "Ok, Grams, I love you". He said, "I love you too cuz, talk to you later".

Before walking away, he says, "I hope you believe in God because everything that he does is sent through signs, pay attention to all of them". Confused, I said, "ok, I will definitely try to". It almost felt like he wanted to tell me something that he had been holding onto but probably did not want to give it away. He took a few steps away from me but then turned back around one last time as he was back stepping and says, *"looking at the ocean waves through a window is the most peaceful sight on earth, it looks even better at night"*. I was so confused by what he had just said. But since he was into music, I just thought that maybe he was repeating a verse from one of his songs. He finally walked away, and I then went back in to sit down and wait my turn.

It was now almost two o'clock and Ashleigh was finally ready for me. She walked over to me and apologized for taking so long to get me in the seat. I told her that it was not a big deal, plus it had given me the chance to catch up with my cousin outside because it had been a while since I had seen or talked to him. She said, "Ok, come on so we can get started". She asked me what I was trying to get done so I pointed at the poster of Rhianna on her wall and told her that I wanted the exact cut and color hair that he had. She laughed and said ok and went on to doing her thing. I knew I was in good hands and I also knew that when I walked out of the salon that day that I was going to look like an entirely different person.

About fifteen-minutes into getting my hair done, I noticed three women walking into the salon. Two of them just sat down on the chairs by the entrance while the girl that had an appointment came and sat at the station right next to the one that I was at. In fact, one of them looked very familiar. She looked like the chick that I had seen pointing at us the night that I was at Mambos with Jeron. These chicks must have been drunk or something because Ashleigh had to tell them at least two times to lower their voices. As they began to get louder again, Ashleigh finally came up with a great idea and just told them to grab their chairs and bring them closer to their friend who was getting her hair done. So, they came with their chairs and moved right between us.

Although they were sitting around each other, they were still talking loudly. I guess it wasn't all that loud because Ashleigh never had to tell them to lower their voices again. These chicks were talking about all kinds of crazy ghetto nonsense. But it wasn't until I had thought that they had said something about a guy named "J" that I began being nosey. They could have been talking about any man nicknamed "J", but I paid closer attention to see if they were really talking about Jeron. And this is what the one sitting closest to me said in what seemed was done all in just one breath.

"I don't know why his bitch ass thought that I was going to answer my phone when he was trying to call like twenty times at two in the morning. Shit, I had to put my phone on silent because I was in the house trying to get my shit off with another dude". And not only that, I was tired of that on and off again shit with him. I wasted so many years waiting for his ass to get out of prison only to end up right back in there every six to seven months. Now I hear he's locked up again for stealing money from the bar that he worked at and that there were inmates in there beatin' his ass over something that he had committed a few years ago and thought he had gotten away with. But you know how the streets are. The streets talk and I think that all the shit he had gotten away with was now finally starting to catch up to him. Speaking of the Devil, this is his mom calling me right now.

I just couldn't believe it. She was a little drunk because I could smell the liquor from where I was sitting at. But I knew that she couldn't have been lying about everything that she was saying because she described the entire situation exactly how it had occurred that night. Now I know for sure she must have been the one that was pointing at us at Mambos. The only thing that concerned me a bit was when she said that he had been getting beat up by the inmates in prison over something that he had done a few years back. I just didn't want to get caught up with anything that he had done or was being accused of doing. And that was probably what his mother was trying to warn me about all along.

I asked Ashleigh if we could take a break so that I could go and use the bathroom really quick. She said "ok, no problem sweetie, I'll be here waiting for you". Bathrooms sort of became my sacFirst the lawyers office and now at the salon. Not to mention, that was where I was at when Jeron ran out of my house too. So,

I went into the bathroom and just took a deep breath then closed my eyes. I wasn't going to go into a prayer to ask God for anything. I just wanted to thank him for guiding me and for opening up my eyes by placing me in front of these current situations that were making me realize that I was just making way too many bad choices in my life. And just like my cousin said to me. *"I hope you believe in God because everything that he does is sent through signs, pay attention to all of them"*. And I truly believed that was for sure one of them.

I also had to thank God for all the ups and downs that I had experienced throughout my life due to them making me a lot stronger. Because if I had been one of those simple types of women that loved to fight over men, I would have jumped out of my chair and stomped the hell out of the one that was saying all those things about Jeron. After taking a few deep breaths and thanking God again for the signs, I made my way back to my station so that Ashleigh could continue doing my hair. As I sat there in a deep thought, it all just started to make sense to me. All I had to do was put everything in God's hands and he would open up my eyes to see things that sex and liquor had been blinding me from.

Looking back at all of the things that I had done to escape the pain from my divorce only seemed to have attracted so many different men who I thought were there to take me away from it all. Instead, all it did was just add another name to the list of men that I have had sex with. The sad part about it though was just when I thought I had finally written down all of the men's names that I had remembered having sex with, there were a few more one-night stands that I had forgotten about. I felt so sorry for myself, but I was determined not to let my past destroy me.

The one thing that I had been blessed with not ever having was any sexually transmitted diseases or being infected with HIV. Although I had protected sex with the majority of the men that I had slept with, I can remember a few times when I was so deep into it that I didn't want to ruin the moment by having to stop to unwrap a condom and mess up the flow of things. Like at the tattoo parlor. I truly believed that God had put me through all those situations so that I could finally reach this point of my life. Because had I not gone through what I did in my past, I would have never learned any of the valuable lessons that were now teaching me to turn into the better person that I was slowly starting to become.

It got to the point where I was feeling guilty for having slept with men who were in relationships because that's not what I wanted to end up dealing with myself. I hated seeing or hearing about women being mentally and physically abused by men. But in most cases, it's because we always ignored all the red flags in the beginning and we allowed certain behavior to continue in fear of losing them. I had to really begin focusing and reminding myself each morning and every night that God always came first. Everything else came second in my life and never the other way around.

Nowhere in that equation was a man going to come between my new relationship with God. Because without the strength that he was now giving me, it was also mentally preparing to be a better mother to my daughter. I'll be damned if I was ever going to just sit back and allow any man to treat her the same way that they had always treated me.

I would never expect anyone to think that because I was trying to change that my past was going to just disappear or that I am going to act as if it never occurred. I guess in a sense what I am trying to prove is that we don't always have to keep punishing ourselves because of it. Like they say, you live and you learn, right? Unfortunately, we become victims to our own ways and assume that what matters most is what people say or think. As if everyone doesn't have a little sexual "*history*" themselves. I hear both men and women who think they are saints saying it all the time. They'll say things like, "You can't turn a hoe into a housewife" or "once a hoe, always a hoe". Crazy thing is that they always seem to only be referring to women when they say that as if a man gets a free pass after being a hoe themselves. Not realizing that being addicted to having sex with so many different partners seemed to always be the main reason why they would always end up lonely in the end. Most sexually addicted people didn't know how to adjust to living or being with just one person.

I had to begin to understand that this world was much bigger than where I lived. I can always try and go somewhere else and just start all over again without worrying about being judged. I mean, how can any man say that women were hoes just because of the things we did with them, but then still try to get with us anyway? To me, they were always the ones who were confused, not us. They were the ones who were never satisfied. They'll lose their soulmate over a one-night-stand and then try to find every excuse in the world to beg their way back.

After we were all done crying and became strong enough again to give them yet another chance, a few months later, they would just cheat all over again. But it was ok when they did it. Not only were we supposed take them back when they cheated, we were also considered hoes for doing the same exact things that they got caught doing. Now you go ahead and try begging a man to take you back after you got caught cheating. Yeah, good luck with that. Not to say that us women were perfect, but I truly believe that women were not only stronger than a man could ever be, we had to put up with a lot more than they could ever deal with.

"Ok Charli, what you think, Ashleigh asked?" "Huh, I quickly snapped myself out of those deep thoughts that I was just having. I was in such a zone that it felt like my haircut only took five minutes. Those deep thoughts seemed to have taken up my entire day. It was very weird. It almost felt like I was having a conversation with myself, to myself, about myself. It's crazy how your mind sort of becomes your own

counselor, yet, we always feel the need to rather hear it from somebody else. I truly began to feel as though most of our thoughts were God's way of trying to communicate with us and since we always seemed to ignore him, he then decided to try to wake us up through the consequences instead.

"Yes, I love it, thank you Ash". "I'm sorry that I barely spoke to you the entire time that I was sitting here, I just went into a deep thought and it almost felt like I wasn't even here". "No problem", said Ash, "I understand trust me". As I began reaching into my purse to pay her for the haircut, she said, *"no charge"*. "What do you mean no charge" I asked her? She said, *trust me, don't worry about it.* After trying a few more times to pay her, she finally convinced me that I didn't have to pay for it. I gave her a quick hug and a kiss on the cheek and made my way towards my car. *"Love you Ashleigh"* I said before leaving. *"Love you too Charli"*, she replied.

Immediately, everything that had occurred at the salon began to replay in my thoughts. I would have probably still been going crazy trying to figure out my situation with Jeron. But the conversation that those girls were having next to me became the biggest sign for me to just leave him for good. Not only that, Jeron's mom was also in contact with them which pretty much told me that Jeron was using all of us to try and get him out of his situations. I was beginning to see and accept that the Jeron had fooled me into believing that he was different. It became clear very fast that he was no

different from any of the other men that I had dealt
with in my past.

Holy Shit

fter getting my haircut, which by the way made me feel amazing, I went home and immediately sat down on the corner of my living room sofa and just stared out my window. My day felt very long, but with everything that happened and all of the things that I heard, I had to take a few minutes to take it all in. First "E" at the office and then the drunk girls at the salon. It was a lot to take in. I really felt like all of it were real signs for me to finally wake up. None of it could have just been a coincidence. I had to do something, and I had to do it now.

I decided that I was going to start listening to my own thoughts and doing what was best for me without second guessing myself like I had always done before. Just the thought of Jeron's case alone was weighing heavily on me. I knew that the process was probably going to take months to handle and that it would probably be me doing all the running around for him. I didn't have the time to be doing all that. Like I said before, I did not ever want to deal with being in a relationship with someone who was locked up in prison. It was way too much to handle and I wanted to get as far away from it as possible. Besides, I just realized that he had been cheating on me all along.

I went into my bedroom, grabbed the box of money and called Jeron's mother. I spoke to her briefly and asked her if it was possible for me to stop by really quick. I even came up with a lie that I had other things to do and that I couldn't stay long. She said "ok" and I was so excited about my decision to just bring Jeron's money back to her that I almost ended up rear-ending someone at a red light. I began feeling lighter and lighter as I got closer to her house. Anyone that has ever dealt with any inmate in the past knows just how much work it is to be running around for them. Doing all of that and then having to work and pay my own bills while they sat up in the prison bored showing each other pictures of their naked girlfriends and probably even gambling off the money that we sent to them, hell no, not me. I worked too hard for my money and I damn sure was not going to be the one sending him any nudes. I've heard too many stories about how those pictures never made their way back out of the prisons.

I finally got to her house, rang the doorbell, and as soon as she opened up the front door, she looked at me as if she didn't recognize me. I then remembered that it was because of my new look. She says, "Oh my God, I love your haircut". I quickly said thank you and just cut her off right there before she even thought about inviting me inside. I didn't want to be rude, but I also didn't want this to take any longer than it needed to take. I told her that my reason for bringing Jeron's money back was because I no longer wanted to take on the responsibility of having to do all the running around for him. Before I could continue with my reason, she says, "trust me, I completely understand, I myself went through the same exact situation with his father". She went on to say that Jeron's father was also into the street life and that, "he was killed right before I gave birth to Jeron". Damn, I know that I said I didn't want to have a conversation, but that damn sure caught my attention.

Although I went over there to just bring the money, somehow, we ended up right back in the living room talking again. I really became curious about Jeron's dad. She asked me if I had a few minutes to spare so she could finish telling me the story. I said yes, I have about thirty minutes before I had to go and meet one of my friends. She said "ok" and immediately jumped right in. Before she got into what happened to Jeron's dad, she told me that I shouldn't feel guilty for not wanting to get involved with Jeron's case. I didn't think that her and I would have been on the same page regarding the situation. But I became comfortable once she started explaining herself.

After about ten minutes on that topic, she then got into talking about Jeron's dad and how he was a big-time drug dealer who had been set up and killed by his own friends down at the Crystal Avenue apartments. Those projects just happen to be the right down the street from where I lived. I hated going down there because them people always acted like you weren't welcome there unless you were from there. I got the point once I read the graffiti on the wall which said, *Crystal Law, Run or be Ran.* That alone gave me the chills. After reading it, the only time that I would go down there was when I had to bring one of my friends to a dealer named Chino that I knew. I would always try to stay in the car though. Chino was an asshole. He never really got over a little joke that I had told another one of my friends about him that till this day, we all still laugh about.

Before I tell you the story, I will be honest with you and tell you that I almost ended up *givin'* it up to him one night. I was drunk at a bar downtown from downing almost half a bottle of Patron and, wait a minute, I had already started to tell you about this story. He was the one that didn't have a condom while we were *grindin'* it up in the alley between the buildings, remember? After that, I had to stop answering his calls because he just wouldn't stop blowing up my phone. I knew that he was just going to end up being a psycho, so I ended up changing my phone number. Anyway, Chino had told me a story once (I believe he was high that day too) about how he always sat down on the toilet to pee because he didn't want to get it all over the bathroom floor and then have to wipe it all down. And for what was that? I just couldn't let it go.

I promised him that I would never share that with anyone, but, of course I did. I just couldn't help it. And he found out all because the girl that I told ended up telling one other dude down at Crystal Avenue and before you knew it, the entire town heard about it and began calling him "Catcher". I guess they came up with that nickname because he used to be a really good baseball player before he chose to sell drugs. It was really sad that he gave up his dreams of being a professional baseball player. That seemed to be the path that most of those great athletes chose to go down at those projects. But I honestly believe that he is still pissed off at me till this day about spreading that rumor about him.

Anyway, so Jeron's mother finally got to the point about the story behind Jeron's scars. Now this is where I began to pay really close attention because it seemed like she was holding back the last time she had brought it up. She began by asking me again, "do you remember the other day when I asked you if you had ever noticed the scars on his face?" I said "yes, of course I remember". I even went home and had a dream about it because it had been on my mind since I left here, I told her. She says, "ok, well let me tell you what happened and then you can leave because I know that you have other things to do".

"Jeron, who you obviously know by now clearly was no saint, had been dealing drugs since he was twelve years old". She went through the entire story about how she found out that he had been dealing drugs and about he began hanging around all types of thugs. She tried to also say a few good things about her son by saying that he was never the type to be disrespectful or the kind who would want to do any harm to anyone. And, I somewhat believed her because he was always respectful towards me and it showed that he had been raised well. He just never once mentioned anything to me about his father, never mind that he had been killed.

You know how Hispanic people are, right? They begin telling you a story about one topic, but then want to start from when they were three years old? In my head I was like, "damn lady, get to the point already". She then finally decided to get to the important part of the story by bringing up the scars again. So, I had to fully concentrate and stop laughing in my thoughts about Chino and the Catcher joke. "Too make a long story short" she says, as if it hadn't already been forty-five minutes, "Jeron had been doing some community service because he was on probation for something petty that he had done".

Then she gets right into how he ended up with the scars. She says, "Jeron had been working at a site where he was using all kinds of tools like hammers, ladders, chainsaws and a whole bunch of other tools, right? I said "ok". And then she says, "the man who killed his father had been released from prison after only doing about twenty something years and that for some reason or another just happened to be walking by the site where Jeron was working at". With my eyes locked into hers, I began to play the entire situation in my own thoughts as if it was all happening right there between us in the living room.

She says, "the man walked up to Jeron and said, you look very familiar for some reason" after asking him if he had a cigarette. She told me that Jeron had come home a little shook up later that day and told her the story about what had happened at the site where he was working at, but that he wasn't the only one who was responsible for it. Now I was very intrigued by the story. I just knew that it was about to get really serious. She continues by saying that, "Jeron told the man that he must be confusing him with somebody else and that the man then responded by saying something like, "you got a slick mouth, just your daddy". Jeron ended up swinging on the man and when the man fell, he had grabbed one of the tools from the floor and hit him across his face with it. She went on to say that Jeron told her that without hesitation, he had then grabbed a hammer and began swinging it on the man and hitting him a few times over the head with it. She then went into how another inmate that had also been working with Jeron just came back from his lunch break and joined in on beating the man up then throwing him in the trunk of Jeron's car.

To get to the point of what occurred that day, she basically ended up telling me that the other man, the one that came back from his lunch break, had just been arrested a few months prior and was out on bond facing twenty years in prison. Instead of just fighting his case in court, he decided to tell the police that he could help them on a cold case that he had known about for many years. The inmate proceeded to tell the detectives that if they drove him to a lake nearby that they would be able to dig up the body of a man that Jeron had killed and then buried. As soon as she told me that part, I immediately knew then that it was the reason why

Jeron was having so many issues in the prison he was at. I didn't know whether to feel sorry for him or to stay as far away from him as I possibly could. Once we were done talking, I noticed that I still had Jeron's money in my hands, so I gave it to her and told her that I had to leave. My body just felt cold and my mind felt completely frozen.

I not only had a thief in my apartment, I was sleeping with a murderer and didn't even know it. I couldn't catch a break. On my back to my apartment, I remembered that I had grabbed a business card from "E" the day I went to go drop off the money at the lawyer's office. I went back and forth in my thoughts on whether I should call him to let him know about what I had just heard or to ask him if we could meet somewhere. I decided to call him, but he did not answer. I left him a voicemail and asked him to please call me back when he had a minute.

Yellow Scooter

s soon as I got home from Jeron's mother's house, I was about to get out of my car when I noticed a man standing on the corner staring at me with a creepy smile. I tried to stay in my car as long as I could hoping that he would just walk away before I got out to make my way into my apartment. After about five minutes of waiting in my car, I decided to just get out and make my way in. As soon as I got out, he slowly began to make his way towards me while pretending that he was texting someone on his phone. Me, knowing how predictable men are when they want something from a woman, I decided to start walking towards him because I didn't want him to know exactly what apartment I lived in. I had my mace already in hand just in case he decided to do something stupid.

After about ten steps, I was now right in front of him. He still had that creepy smile on his face. He says, *hey, how are you beautiful*?" Now you already know how felt about that word, but this time, I didn't want to risk anything with this man because he did look a little crazy. So, I said, "I'm good", but did not go any further by asking him how he was doing. I didn't want to give him the impression that we were going to be standing there having a conversation. I always knew that anytime you ever replied to a man that they would automatically assume that you were interested in them. And that's why I always ignored most of them.

He then asked me, "if I gave you my number, would you call me?" I said, "No". He, without waiting first to see if I had anything else to say besides just saying "no" quickly gets pissed off and then says to me, "well fuck you then bitch, you ain't all that anyway". It was funny as hell. Not because he had just cursed me out, but because as I stood there shocked by his response, he sped walked back to the corner where he had been standing at and then jumped on his yellow mini-scooter and rode off honking his horn at me with his middle finger up in the air. I almost passed out laughing.

As much as he tried to be disrespectful, I felt like I really needed that laugh. I then walked into my apartment and as soon as I opened up my refrigerator to grab a Pepsi, my phone rings. It was "E" returning my call. I answered, "hello" he then began apologizing for missing my call and that he had been on the phone with the nurse who was taking care of his ailing mother at a convalescent home in Connecticut. As much as I wanted to ask him about the condition of his mother, I instead asked "Connecticut?" He said, "yea, that's where I'm originally from and although I loved New York, I might have to move back there to be by her side as much as I could". I said, "oh wow, ok", before saying sorry to him about his mother.

I told him that maybe I should call him back some other time because I felt that since he was dealing with his mother's situation that it was far more important than what I had to tell him. He said, "no, that's ok, what's going on?" That one question led us to be on the phone till almost four in the morning. Somehow, after I told him about Jeron's situation, we ended up talking about things that had nothing to do with the case. In fact, he acted like he didn't even care about Jeron's situation because all he said was, "yea, I've dealt with so many cases throughout my years that nothing surprises me anymore". I felt stupid for a minute because I thought he was going to be all over it. But that's like expecting a nurse in a trauma unit at a hospital crying over a victim who somehow accidentally cut up half of his face with a chainsaw. Yeah, I know, bad example but you know what I mean, right?

I felt so good after we hung up. It had been a long time since I had spent almost the entire night talking to a man on the phone. And "E" and I weren't even dating which made it even more interesting. I know that I am trying to clean myself up and straighten out my behavior, but I have to admit, I did end up touching myself while I was on the phone with him. I thought that he had heard me moan because he asked me "are you ok" right in the middle of talking to me about something else. I played it off and said, "yea, I'm ok, I was just reaching across the bed for my soda". I don't think he believed me because he then said while chuckling a little, "Oh, ok, I thought it sounded like it was *something else*". I tried flirting back by asking him, "well, what do you think it sounded like?" But being the respectful man that he was, he said, "never mind" while still chuckling and continued on with his conversation.

Before we hung up the phone and went to sleep, he asked if I could stop by the office sometime "this week". I told him that I would try to, but that if I couldn't do it this week that I would definitely go the following week. Lord knows I wanted to say yes. But I had to work all week and I really didn't have the time to go and see him. He said, "oh, ok no problem" and told me to just keep him posted on whenever I could stop by. The funny thing was that he never really gave me any reason as to why he wanted me to stop by, but I never asked him either. Besides, I forgot to mention to him that I had already made plans to go see my family in Connecticut over the weekend.

After having such a rough week between work and all the rest of the crazy things that I had been dealing with, I was finally happy to be in Connecticut with my family. It felt great to be away from all the drama. I wanted to go out and have some fun, so we bought tickets for Julia to see *Laura Dowding* in concert at the Mohegan Sun Casino. I knew that she would love it because she knows all the words to her platinum selling single *"You Matter"*. Julia is my daughter's name. In fact, I named her after my grandmother who always took care of me for most of my life because my mother was barely ever around. Now that I think about it, I kind of wonder if my mother had similar issues as to the ones that I am currently dealing with in my life today? Anyway, the concert was great, and Julia seemed to have had the time of her life.

I promised myself that I was not going to be all over social media or spend too much time on the phone because I wanted my daughter to have all my attention. I hated being around other people who were always stuck on their phones caring more about their likes and less about their kids. But later that night, once my daughter had fallen already fallen asleep, I went to go and take a shower so that I could get in bed myself. I had brought my phone with me because I needed to use the flashlight in the hallway, and I didn't want to wake my daughter up by turning on the lights. The bathroom was right next to the bedroom where she was sleeping at so I wanted to hurry up and take a shower as fast as I could. Once I walked into the bathroom, I immediately turned the shower on. I took a quick peek at my phone to see if I had any missed calls, but instead I noticed that I had a few text messages instead.

I tried to rush through my shower, but I just felt dirty from having been out all day. And you know how us women with all the nice curves and pretty faces are. We took showers like we were expecting to meet our soul mates in our dreams. Well, at least that's how I always felt. I even wore nice panties to sleep because you know what they always say, right? "Oh, you don't?" Well let me help you out with that. My grandmother would always tell us that we had to make sure that we wore clean underwear because you just never knew if you were going to be in an accident. But the only "accidents" that I had ever been in while involving my panties were the men that always helped me take them off.

After about twenty-minutes, I finally turned the shower off, dried myself and then grabbed my phone. With one towel wrapped around my body and another one on my head, I sat on top of the toilet seat to see who it was that had been messaging me. All three messages were from "E". One of them said, "Hey", the second one said, "Are you busy" and the third one said, "text me back when you have a minute". I immediately thought there was something wrong with his mother and that he needed someone to talk to. Although it had already been a little over an hour ago since he had messaged me, I text him back hoping that he was still up. I was so quick with responding to his message because I didn't want him to think that I was out with another man. And again, we weren't even dating. But I didn't want to ruin anything in case there really was going to be a future between us.

As soon as I sent my message, I saw those three little dots that you see when someone is responding so I knew that he was still up. He asked me if I could talk. I told him that I had just gotten out of the shower and was about to put on my pajamas and that I would call him in a few. He texted back "ok". I had to go into my mom's car which was parked in the garage to talk to him because I didn't want to wake anyone up. Once I heard the tone of his voice, I knew that it wasn't about anything serious. He was really calm and he sounded as sexy as he always did. I never wanted to tell him this but hearing his voice while picturing his face always made me feel like I was really talking to Idris Elba. I didn't know how he would feel about me saying that, so I never mentioned it.

About ten minutes into our conversation, he mentioned that people always tell him that he looks like Idris. After asking him again to repeat to me what he had just said because I pretended like I didn't hear him the first time, I asked him, "who, Idris Elba? He said, "yea, you know the actor?" I said, "boy please" and he just started laughing. I thought it was weird that he had brought it up since I was just literally thinking about that myself. So, from that moment on, I nicknamed him Idris and he just went along with it.

I thought it was odd that he never once asked me where I was at. I was so used to feeling like I was on parole or probation anytime that I dated someone that I was expecting him to ask me those same types of questions. But again, he was such a gentleman and I never sensed that he would be like any man that I had ever dealt with. We spoke for about two hours before he reminded me again about trying to come by the office whenever I could. I said "ok" and before I hung up the phone I almost slipped and said "I love you" which would have really been embarrassing. We finally hung up and I went back inside the house to wash my hands and change my soaked silk pink panties.

Ailing Mother

I finally ended meeting up with "E" later that week after having an amazing time with family over the weekend. I would have gone sooner, but I didn't want to make it seem like I was desperate to go see him. I waited until Thursday to go down to his office. It was five days after he had reminded me about coming to see him, but we had been talking on the phone every day before I finally saw him again. "E" would always send me random text messages through-out the days which made me wonder if it was because I was on his mind or because he just felt like he needed someone to talk to outside of his stressful job and ailing mother.

I wasn't sure, but either way, I was enjoying our friendship. In fact, he had me checking my phone almost every minute just to see if he had messaged me. And to be honest, even if he wasn't trying to get with me, I'd much rather talk to him about anything over the phone than to go back to talking to anyone who would remind me of the men that I had dealt with in the past. He really made me feel comfortable. He was very respectful, funny and if I hadn't mentioned it to you before, he was *fine* as hell too.

He told me that he had taken some personal time off because he wanted to go and visit his mother in Connecticut. I felt so bad for him. I wish that there was something I could do for him, but I didn't feel as though it was my place to ask him questions about her, but I did want him to know that I was really concerned about him. So, I came up with an even better idea. I went online and got his mother a gift card to *Filomena's Restaurant* which was right there in the same area and just down the street from the convalescent home where she was a resident at. I knew that she couldn't leave the facility, but "E" could just go by and pick some food then bring it to her when he stopped by to visit her.

Things had been going smooth compared to all the things that I had been going through the past few months. "E" and I continued getting to know each other better by the day and other than me reaching out to my girlfriends every once in a while to catch up, I pretty much just went to work and hung around my apartment watching Netflix by myself. I no longer felt the urge or the need to be clubbin' or hanging out in places that would only remind me of the person I no longer wanted to be. I tried going to the gym a few times just to keep my mind off of things, but the of men there were sometimes worse than the men at the bars. Every five seconds there was a man in front either staring at me or asking me if I needed help. Days turned into weeks and weeks turned into months and finally the day of Jeron's sentencing came up.

Although "E" was still representing him as his lawyer, him and I had become sort of like *best friends*.

I'm not sure how much effort he had put into the case or how it was going because after I had dropped the money off to Jeron's mother, I had made "E" promise me that we would not have any conversations about it anymore. He agreed and never brought it to until the day of the sentencing. He said that the only reason why he mentioned anything about the case to me was because he was happy that the day had finally come.

Before heading out and driving down to the courthouse, he texted me to let me know he might be there most of the day because he had two different inmates to represent and it just happened to be both of their sentencing dates. He told me that although his day was looking like it was going to be very long, that he was happy about it because he could finally be able to concentrate a lot more on his future plans. He never mentioned to me about what those plans were, but I just replied "ok" and told him that I hoped he had a great day and to text me once he was done with work.

Later that evening, he called to tell me that he was finally heading home from court but that he had to stop by his office to drop off all of his paperwork and then head out to have a drink. For the first time since we had become friends, I asked him if he minded if I could join him. I was a bit nervous when I asked him, but even more nervous about thinking that he might say "no". Without pausing to even think about it, he said, "I would love that, I'll even come by and pick you up". I was so excited. I went and took a shower, got ready and waited for him to come get me.

We stopped by *The Green Room* to go see and have a quick drink with my friend Tondra, then after about an hour or so, we headed down to *The Bank at 12* which was right down the street and around the corner from *Thames Landing.* I loved it there. The owners Mike and Des always took care of us ever time that we stopped by. After having a few drinks there, he began to open up a little more about his mother's condition and told me that she had been getting worse. He reminded me again that he might have to move soon to be a little closer in order to be there for her. In my head I was thinking, "damn, why is it that every time I get closer to someone, something always had to happen where they ended up leaving me somehow". I was broken inside, but I could not show him that side of me because we were only friends.

After a few more drinks, I felt like he had just shattered me inside like I did my mirror that day. He told me that he was planning on moving to Connecticut by March 24th, which was only about two weeks away. I tried to hold back, but I ended up making a fool of myself and began crying right there in front of him. He came and sat closer to me placed his arm around my back to try and calm me down. I was sitting there crying into my hands while he whispered, "I'm sorry Charli, I'm really sorry" in my ear. I ended up crying for the rest of the night.

Ice Cubes

ut in, I whispered. Just slide my panties to the side but please take your time *baby,* don't rush it. I was laying with my head sideways on the pillow so he could hear me moaning softly into his ear. *Like that baby, please don't stop baby.* He kept saying over and over that he loved the way my pussy felt. *"Is this my pussy baby, he asked?"* I responded to him, *"Yes, baby, "this is your pussy daddy".* I kept closing my eyes but would open them wide as he slid deeper and deeper inside me. He then turned me around and asked me to spread my legs wide so he could see himself going in and out of me. I could see from the corner of my left eye that he was really into me. Every five or six strokes, he had to slow himself down to keep himself from cumin' too fast.

I was so deep in thought while he gave it to me slowly from behind. I hadn't had sex since I had gotten my tattoo and I felt like a virgin all over again as he went deeper into my tight pussy. I was so wet that I could hear him sliding it in and out of me. I could tell that he loved it when I looked back to watch him *fuckin'* me. After having to stop a few more times, he then laid on his back and wanted me to get on top. Oh my God, I was ridin' him so good that it seemed as if his eyes were rolling to the back of his head. I slowed down because I didn't want him to finish before I got mine off first.

I placed my chest on top of his and slowed all the way down while riding just the tip of his dick. He was going crazy. I felt him shakin' a few times as if he was trying to hold back. I was doing it just right. Once I felt like his tip was about to slide out, I went all the way down as far as I could and just held it there and then rode my pussy all the way back up slowly. I then moved up and whispered in his ear to stay right where he was at on the bed and not to move. Before walking out of the bedroom, I looked back and caught him staring at my ass like he wanted more.

I walked into my kitchen and grabbed my tin New York Yankees cup and filled it up with ice cubes. I then made my way back into the bedroom as fast as I could so that his dick wouldn't go soft on me. I grabbed an ice cube and placed it in my mouth while he just stared at me. You can tell that he was a little nervous about what I was about to do to him. I began by lickin' on his neck with my cold lips and worked my way down to his chest. I was making him feel so good that I could tell that his toes were curling up just by the way his legs became tighter and tighter. I had him just where I wanted. He had been sweating all over me and I was now cooling him off with the cubes.

I then began jerking him off with my right hand while I reached to grab another piece from the cup with my left. Once I had placed another cube in my mouth, I gave him one last look before I started licking around and between the inside of his legs. He was going crazy. When I felt that the ice was getting smaller, I lifted his dick up with my left hand and just began to lick on his balls. He curled up like a baby and couldn't even talk. I went through the entire cup. The ice had him on cloud nine.

I came back up to his ear again and asked him if he wanted me to stop. He just looked at me and before he could even answer, I had already placed another cube in my mouth and began licking on his tip. I have never seen a man go crazier than the way I was making him feel on my bed. His fingers were locked in my hair so tight that he was pulling me back every time he felt he couldn't take it anymore. I then started to play with myself at the same time that I was sucking his dick and suddenly, I began to hear "E" whispering, *Charliii, Charliii....* I whispered back saying *yes baby...this feels so good.* And then I heard E again whispering a little louder saying *Charliiii, Charliiii... I whispered again, yes daddy, yesss.* Then I heard "E" saying, *Charli, wake up.* What??? Wake up, you've dreaming and moaning out loud for the past ten minutes and you woke me up. Once he noticed that I was up, he then walked right back into the living room.

It was all a dream that I had been having with "E", but it had felt so real. How was I going to look him in his face when I came out of my bedroom in the morning? I then wondered what I had been saying out loud throughout my dream and how much he had heard. I wanted to just lay there and never come out. I looked at my phone and it was only six in the morning. Not only was I embarrassed, I was so out of it that I couldn't even remember why "E" was even there. And then it hit me, he had spent the night and slept in the living room because I had been crying since we left the restaurant. Oh my God.... How was I going to explain myself to him about this dream that I was just having? I got up and walked into my bathroom to wipe myself up then just rolled myself back into my comforter and went back to sleep. I was so embarrassed.

The Night Before

I can't believe that two weeks had already passed since "E" told me that he was moving to Connecticut. I felt like I needed to be put on some type of medication to help control my nerves. I had never experienced this much stress in my life. As a matter of fact, it felt worse than my divorce and Jeron's situation put together times ten. He was moving to Connecticut, which was only a little over two hours away. But it just wasn't going to be feel the same. I was devastated.

Getting to really know "E" all this time had made me feel like him and I should have already been together in a relationship. But he was now leaving in just a few hours. The night he told me that he was moving, he had asked me to take three personal days off from my job. He told me to make sure that the days that I took off started on the same day that he was going to be moving which meant he had wanted me to take an entire weekend off.

I was so happy that I had at least spent almost every single day with "E" leading up to the day that he was going to leave. We had just continued with our normal routine of talking on the phone and going out for drinks. On his last night in Brooklyn, he had asked if he could spend the night. I was nervous to say yes because you know what had already occurred two weeks ago. He never did bring that up to me although he did laugh a little when he asked if he could stay over again. I told him that I didn't mind if he stayed. In my thoughts, I really would have loved it if he would just come in my room and we did everything that I had dreamt about. But I was not going to push myself onto him. I had way too much respect for him.

"E" was very good to me throughout our entire friendship. Although I wish that sometimes he would just come out of his shell and just jumped all over me, I was also ok with him just being a great friend. At least I knew I had a friend in him and not just hanging out with another man that would just treat me like the rest of them already had. He had come over several times in the past, but we sat around and talked about random things or sometimes he would just grab the remote and watch different sports or ESPN. Every time I saw that it was a baseball game, it would always remind me of *Chino's* joke. I laughed about it each and every time like it was always the first time I had ever heard it.

It started to get later, and I knew that "E" had to get ready for bed soon because he had to take that long ride to Connecticut in the morning. I told him that I was going to take a shower and get ready for bed and that I would leave a towel and washrag in the bathroom for him. He said "ok" and then continued watching the Yankees preseason game until I was done in the bathroom. When I came out to let him know that I was done, I noticed that he had already fallen asleep. At first, I was in my robe. But when I noticed that he hadn't seen me in it, I quickly went into my room and put on my tight little *boy-shorts* with a tight white t-shirt where he could see my nipples through.

I went up to him and tapped him on his leg a few times while calling his name and after the fourth time, he finally woke up. Typical "E", he didn't even notice that I was basically trying to turn him on by what I was wearing. He said "ok" and got up to take his shower. I felt a little stupid, but I wasn't really expecting him to rip me out of my clothes anyway. It was a nice try, but I didn't feel any type of way towards him just because of that. He went and took his shower and before heading back into the living room, he said, "*goodnight*" and just went about his business. I just laughed in my thoughts.

Leaving Brooklyn

he next morning came really fast. I slept through the entire night without anything crazy or embarrassing happening this time. When he woke up, he didn't even act like it was his last day. He was just being himself as usual. He looked outside through my living room window and made a joke like, "well, at least the U-Haul is still parked outside" and then smiled and chuckled a little bit. I guess he was trying to insinuate that I lived in the bad side of town, but I did think it was a little funny the way he said it. But other than that comment, he seemed unbothered and very comfortable. The only thing that I found was a little funny was that he waited until the day of to tell, *not ask me*, that he needed me to drive his car and follow him in the U-Haul down to Connecticut.

He told me not to worry because he was going to be driving me back home after we were all done with unloading the truck. I guess that's why he needed me to take those days off. I didn't have an issue with it though. It actually made me feel better that I wasn't just going to be saying good-bye to him in my living room like I had been picturing in my thoughts. I felt really sad but continued on with getting ready to leave. I packed extra clothes just in case. In fact, I packed like I was going away for an entire week. He went and got ready himself. I had scrambled some eggs and made us coffee so that we could have a little breakfast before heading out.

Finally, we left my apartment by ten a.m. After being on the highway for about an hour, I noticed that he had put his blinker on to pull over into the McDonalds on the right. Once we parked, he came over to tell me that he couldn't hold it anymore and had to go and use the bathroom really quick. When he came back, I noticed that he had bought me my favorite candy, which was peanut M&M's and a Pepsi. He jumped into the car with me for a few minutes. After a few seconds, I noticed that someone was trying to call him. I kept hearing his phone vibrating and then I saw his phone flashing through his sweatpants pocket. He took it out, looked at it, and then ended the call. But before he ended it, I noticed that on the dash of his car monitor that it had said incoming call from Grams.

I thought nothing of it. I just assumed that he also knew someone by the name of Grams so I never did ask him. I did not want him to think that I was the nosey type and I damn sure wasn't going to get into a discussion that could lead to an argument on our last few days of hanging out together. I wanted everything to be as peaceful as it had always been between us. Once we got back on the highway, it did remind me to call my cousin Grams just to check on him. Yes, I did want to see if maybe it was him that had called "E", but I wasn't going to make it that obvious by just coming out and asking him. He never did answer though. So, I just left him a voicemail to call me back.

After being on the highway for a few hours, we finally made it to Waterford, Connecticut which happened to be the city right next to where my mother and daughter lived in New London. We got there around one-thirty due to a little traffic and not to mention how slow he was driving the U-Haul. But as tired as we were and after taking about a twenty-minute break while sitting in the front seat of his car, we finally decided to get out and walk towards the house. For some reason, I thought he was renting it, but when he asked, "You like it?" "I got it for a lot cheaper than I expected to pay for it". It was gorgeous. And when I walked through the living room and into the kitchen, I looked out the window that was right above the kitchen sink and saw just how beautiful the ocean view was. I felt like I was staring at heaven.

I was so happy for him. After having a quick conversation with him about the house, we decided that we had to get to work and start bringing in everything that he had in the truck. Five minutes in and his phone began ringing but it was out loud this time. When he answered it, and I heard him say, "I can't talk right now *bro*, I'm a little busy, but I'll call you back later". He then hung up the phone and got right back to bringing the boxes into his house. I didn't think anything of the phone call since he called the person "bro". I'm not going to lie, I honestly thought that a man with all that money and with the house that he had just purchased, that it was a matter of time before he did find a woman in the neighborhood to be with being that he was the new man in town.

My phone was now ringing and when I looked, it was my cousin Grams. I had answered the phone on speaker because I wanted to keep working on unloading the truck and didn't want to slow down. "E" heard our entire conversation and when I hung up, he asked me, "you know a guy name Grams too?" I said, "yea, he's my cousin, why you ask?" He just said that he also knew someone by that name but that he was sure that it couldn't be the same person. Once again, I left it at that because he had heard my cousins voice through the speaker and didn't react like he had recognized it. So, we went on and continued unloading the truck. I suddenly began to notice that some of the boxes said *his* while others said *hers* written in marker. I thought maybe they belonged to his mom, but then I remembered that she was in a convalescent home. I'm not even going to lie. I was a little confused, but I was also a little upset about it.

After taking a few minutes to collect my thoughts, I went right back to work. I leaned in to go and grab the next thing closest to me in the truck when suddenly the weirdest things just happened to enter my thoughts. Those thoughts began racing even more as soon as I had put both of my hands on the *mirror* that I had grabbed to bring inside. After taking a few steps, I had to stop because my *tattoo* started itching really bad out of nowhere. While I was pulling up my shirt to let the wind cool it off, I looked into the house and "*E*" was in there taking things out of the boxes. It couldn't be. I honestly thought I was going crazy. "E" which just happened to be the last letter missing from my tattoo, began to feel like it was yet another sign from God. It all started making more and more sense to me right away.

I started thinking back to when "E" had asked me if I was in a relationship or if I was single before asking me if I believed in God right before I walked out of his office the first time that we met. Then, I remembered when Grams had told me that "*looking at the ocean waves through a window is the most peaceful sight on earth, it looks even better at night*". I didn't want to believe it, but I even began to feel different inside. I thought at that moment that God was really messing with me since I had always been asking him to give me hints from the time I had broken my mirror on my bedroom floor. And holy shit, it was right after I touched that mirror that I began to have these thoughts. Could all this really be a sign? I didn't want to just ignore it. Not only that, it seemed like he had waited for Jeron to get sentenced to move out of state. Funny thing was that he still hadn't even brought up anything about his mother. I know, I'm probably just overthinking all these things and that probably none of it was even connected somehow. I closed my eyes for about two minutes and prayed,

Please God, please let it be that this man has brought me out here to Connecticut to make me his wife. Please let it be that all of these signs that are making me feel this way are all real. I know that I have been through a lot and I am sorry God that I never did turn to you for help. I promise you that if this situation is what I'm really thinking in my head that I will never turn my back on you my dear God. Please let "E" be the man that you have chosen for me. In your name I pray dear God, Amen.

Ocean View

fter ending my prayer, I felt so relieved that I was no longer bothered about the *his* and *hers* written on the boxes that I had been carrying in. Once I had opened up my eyes from praying, I started to make my way back into the house with the mirror in my hand. I noticed that it was really quiet. I walked around looking for "E" and couldn't find him anywhere. I started to call his name, but no response. It was a really big house, but "E" was nowhere to be found. He never mentioned anything to me about going anywhere and his car was still outside in the front, so I knew that he had to be somewhere near. I thought maybe he had met one of the new neighbors out back. I went back downstairs and started to call out his name. Again, no response from him.

I went back out front and grabbed my cell phone from inside the truck to try and call him. I called him twice, but both times it went to his voicemail. Now I started to worry about him. I went next door to see if maybe the neighbors had seen him and after introducing myself to them, they said that they hadn't seen him either. I went back to the house and just sat down on the floor for a few minutes. I began to have that abandoned feeling again. I closed my eyes again and just said a quick prayer. *"Please, God, I hope that everything is ok with him, Amen"*.

I stood back up and walked into the kitchen. It was almost eight pm and it was a little dark outside. I stopped and stared through the window above the sink towards the ocean view out back. It was really beautiful and peaceful. Then, I thought maybe "E" had received a phone call and just decided to take a quick walk on the beach to have his conversation. I hoped that everything was ok with his mother and that nothing had happened to her. My thoughts were just all over the place.

Finally, I go rushing down the stairs through the back door. You are not going to believe what I saw. After all this time that I had been running around looking for "E", he had been waiting for me quietly the entire time right under the kitchen deck out back. I made it to the bottom of the steps and I just began to cry hysterically. I looked around and saw E's parents, all of his friends, my mother, my beautiful daughter, my girlfriends from back home, and of all people, my cousin Grams with a big ol' smile on his face. Even Ashleigh made it down. And right there in front of all of them was "E" on one knee holding onto a small burgundy box with a beautiful diamond ring inside. *"Will you marry me?"* I yelled out in excitement, *"Oh my God"*, I ran up to "E" and as he was standing back up from proposing to me and just jumped right into his arms. I was so excited that I didn't even have the time to say *"YES"*. I just put my left hand out in front of him while he put my new beautiful diamond engagement ring on my ring finger. I just couldn't stop crying.

"E" had made them park around the corner and then snuck them through the back of the house while I was still unloading. My friends and family had known all along. After saying "Yes", we all went back upstairs and began telling stories. "E" came out first apologizing and saying that he couldn't have come up with a better "*lie*" than the one that he had come up with about his mother. He said that when he came up with it, that he had just gotten off the phone with her and it was the first thing that had popped into his head. The times that he had been telling me that he was traveling to Connecticut was to try to buy our new house.

Then, remember when my girlfriends showed up to my apartment right after my situation with Jeron? They had already heard about the rumors that were going around town about Jeron messing with one of those three girls that were at the salon the day of my appointment. I didn't realize it then, but I understand now why they felt the need to come around more. Had it not been for them, I probably would have gone crazy. They never wanted to tell me what they knew because they didn't think it was the right time to tell me. Besides, my cousin Grams had been keeping all of them in loop of things and told them to just come and keep me company.

After I had left the office the day of my appointment, "E" had called Grams and asked him if he knew a woman by the name "*Charli*" and explained to him that I was on my way to the hair salon. Grams told him that he had a cousin named "*Charli*" and that if he wanted to make sure that they were talking about the same person that he would go down to the salon and check. "E" said, "*ok, but if it is her, please make sure to pay the hair stylist for the haircut and then you can just come by my office and I will pay you back*". Grams saw that it was me who they had been talking about and he went on to pay Ashleigh without me knowing. Even Ashleigh was in on it. I couldn't believe it. She said that she didn't know those girls or what they had been talking about, but that she was happy that I heard everything that they were saying because I didn't need to be with a man like Jeron anyway.

Grams had already called my mom and told her that she did not need to worry about me because he was "*hooking*" me up with a great man and that I would be moving to Connecticut soon. Now the crazy part was that the entire time that "E" was hiding the fact that he knew my cousin Grams, I had no idea that they were all staying in contact with each other about all these plans. Remember, Grams told me to trust in God and that he works through signs. Which was almost the same thing that "E" was trying to say to me right before I had walked out of his office that day.

It was so beautiful. We had such a great time. And Grams was right. The ocean view was very beautiful at night. I was now going to be looking at it every night as "E" and I were engaged and now living together. Not only does God work in mysterious ways, time and patience is the key to everything in life. My life was complete. I was now living in Waterford right next to my mother. I called my job the next day and told them that I was sorry, but that I had moved out of state with my now future husband. Even the knew about it. "E" had already contacted them as well which was the reason why they never gave me an issue about asking for those three days off with such short notice. We ended celebrating our engagement at Filomena's Restaurant where we were finally able to use that gift card that I had bought for E's mother. What a night. What a life...Thank you God!!!

Love Charli...

Coming Soon...

His side of the story.

Valentine's Day 2020